"Why do you think your father wouldn't be in there?"

How could I possibly explain it?

Dr. Botnick looked at me as though she really wanted to help. But even in my own head it sounded insane. I couldn't tell her about the Bat Lady, who may be Lizzy Sobek, the Holocaust hero everyone thought had died in World War II. I couldn't tell her about the Abeona Shelter, the secret society that rescued children, and how Ema, Spoon, Rachel, and I had risked our lives in its service. I couldn't tell her about that creepy paramedic with the sandy hair and green eyes, the one who took my father away and then, eight months later, tried to kill me.

Who would believe such crazy talk?

Uncle Myron saw me squirm in my seat. "The reasons are confidential," he said, trying to come to my rescue. "Would you please just tell us what you found in the casket?"

Dr. Botnick started chewing on the end of her pen. We waited.

Finally, Myron tried again: "Is my brother in the casket, yes or no?"

She put the pen down on her desk and stood.

"Why don't you come with me and see for yourself?"

ALSO BY HARLAN COBEN

Shelter

Seconds Away

HARLAN COBEN

FOUND

MICKEY BOLITAR BOOK 3

speak

SPEAK
An imprint of Penguin Random House LLC
375 Hudson Street
New York, New York 10014

First published in the United States of America by G. P. Putnam's Sons,
a division of Penguin Young Readers Group, 2014
Published by Speak, an imprint of Penguin Random House LLC, 2015

LIBRARY OF CONGRESS CATALOGING-IN-PUBLICATION DATA IS AVAILABLE.

Speak ISBN 978-0-14-751574-2

Printed in the United States of America

1 3 5 7 9 10 8 6 4 2

To the A Dorm Boys

Brad Bradbeer
Curk Burgess
Jon Carlson
Larry Vitale

Four men who lived with me.
And survived.

CHAPTER 1

Eight months ago, I watched my father's coffin being lowered into the ground. Today I was watching it being dug back up.

My uncle Myron stood next to me. Tears ran down his face. His brother was in that coffin—no, strike that, his brother was *supposed* to be in that coffin—a brother who *supposedly* died eight months ago, but a brother Myron hadn't seen in twenty years.

We were at the B'nai Jeshurun Cemetery in Los Angeles. It was not yet six in the morning, so the sun was just starting to rise. Why were we here so early? Exhuming a body, the authorities had explained to us, upsets people. You need to do it at a time of maximum privacy. That left late at night—uh, no thank you—or very early in the morning.

Uncle Myron sniffled and wiped his eye. He looked as

1

though he wanted to put his arm around me, so I slid a little farther away. I stared down at the dirt. Eight months ago, the world had held such promise. After a lifetime of traveling overseas, my parents decided to settle back in the United States so that I, as a sophomore in high school, would finally have real roots and real friends.

It all changed in an instant. That was something I had learned the hard way. Your world doesn't come apart slowly. It doesn't gradually crumble or break into pieces. It can be destroyed in a snap of the fingers.

So what happened?

A car crash.

My father died, my mother fell apart, and in the end, I was made to live in New Jersey with my uncle, Myron Bolitar. Eight months ago, my mother and I came to this very cemetery to bury the man we loved like no other. We said the proper blessings. We watched as the coffin was lowered into the ground. I even threw ceremonial dirt on my father's grave.

It was the worst moment of my life.

"Stand back, please."

It was one of graveyard workers. What did they call someone who worked in a graveyard? *Groundskeeper* seemed too tame. *Gravedigger* seemed too creepy. They had used a bulldozer to bring up most of the dirt. Now these two guys in overalls—let's call them groundskeepers—finished with their shovels.

Uncle Myron wiped the tears from his face. "Are you okay, Mickey?"

I nodded. I wasn't the one crying here. He was.

A man wearing a bow tie and holding a clipboard frowned and took notes. The two groundskeepers stopped digging. They tossed their shovels out the hole. The shovels landed with a *clank*.

"Done!" one shouted. "Securing it now."

They started shimmying nylon belts under the casket. This took some doing. I could hear their grunts of exertion. When they finished, they both jumped out of the hole and nodded toward the crane operator. The crane operator nodded back and pulled a lever.

My father's casket rose out of the earth.

It had not been easy to arrange this exhumation. There are so many rules and regulations and procedures. I don't really know how Uncle Myron pulled it off. He has a powerful friend, I know, who helped ease the way. I think maybe my best friend Ema's mother, the Hollywood star Angelica Wyatt, may have used her influence too. The details, I guess, aren't important. The important thing was, I was about to learn the truth.

You are probably wondering why we are digging up my father's grave.

That's easy. I needed to be sure that Dad was in there.

No, I don't think that there was a clerical error or that he was put in the wrong coffin or buried in the wrong spot. And, no, I don't think my dad is a vampire or a ghost or anything like that.

I suspect—and, yes, it makes no sense at all—that my father may still be alive.

It particularly makes no sense in my case because I was in that car when it crashed. I saw him die. I saw the paramedic shake his head and wheel my father's limp body away.

Of course, I had also seen that same paramedic try to kill me a few days ago.

"Steady, steady."

The crane began to swing toward the left.

It lowered my father's casket onto the back of a pickup truck. His coffin was a plain pine box. This, I knew, my father would have insisted upon. Nothing fancy. My father wasn't religious, but he loved tradition.

After the coffin touched down with a quiet thud, the crane operator turned off the engine, jumped out, and hurried toward the man with the bow tie. The operator whispered something in the man's ear. Bow Tie looked back at him sharply. The crane operator shrugged and walked away.

"What do you think that was about?" I asked.

"I have no idea," Uncle Myron said.

I swallowed hard as we started toward the back of the pickup truck. Myron and I stepped in unison. That was a little weird. Both of us are tall—six foot four inches. If the name Myron Bolitar rings a bell, that could be because you're a basketball fan. Before I was born, Myron was an All-American collegiate player at Duke and then was chosen in the first round of the NBA draft by the Boston Celtics. In his very first preseason game—the first time he got to wear his Celtic green uniform—an opposing player named Burt Wesson smashed into Myron, twisting my uncle's knee and ending his career before it began. As a basketball player myself—one who hopes to surpass his uncle—I often wonder what that must have been like, to have all your hopes and dreams right there, right at your fingertips, wearing that green uniform you always dreamed would be yours and then, *poof,* it was all gone in a crash.

Then again, as I looked at the casket, I thought that maybe I already knew.

Like I said before, your world can change in an instant.

Uncle Myron and I stopped in front of the coffin and lowered our heads. Myron sneaked a glance at me. He, of course, didn't believe that my father was still alive. He had agreed to do this because I asked—begged, really—and he was trying to "bond" with me by humoring my request.

The pine casket looked rotted, fragile, as though it might collapse if we just looked at it too hard. The answer was right there, feet in front of me. Either my dad was in that box or he wasn't. Simple when you put it that way.

I moved a little closer to the casket, hoping to feel something. My father was supposed to be in that box. Shouldn't

I . . . I don't know . . . feel something if that were the case? Shouldn't there be a cold hand on my neck or a shiver down my spine?

I felt neither.

So maybe Dad wasn't in there.

I reached out and rested my hand on the lid of the casket.

"What do you think you're doing?"

It was Bow Tie. He had introduced himself to us as an environmental health inspector, but I had no idea what that meant.

"I was just . . ."

Bow Tie moved between my father's casket and me. "I explained to you the protocol, didn't I?"

"Well, yes, I mean . . ."

"For reasons of both public safety and respect, no casket can be opened on these premises." He talked as if he were reading an SAT reading comprehension section out loud. "This county transport vehicle will bring your father's casket to the medical examiner's office, where it will be opened by a trained professional. That is my job here—to make sure that we have opened the correct grave, to make sure the casket matches the public records on the person being exhumed, to make sure that all proper health measures have been taken, and finally to make sure that the transport goes smoothly and respectfully. So if you don't mind . . ."

I looked at Myron. He nodded. I slowly lifted my hand off the soggy, dirty pine. I took a step back.

"Thank you," Bow Tie said.

The crane operator was whispering now with a grounds-keeper. The groundskeeper's face turned white. I didn't like that. I didn't like it at all.

"Is something wrong?" I asked Bow Tie.

"What do you mean?"

"I mean, what's with all the whispering?"

Bow Tie started studying his clipboard as though it held some special answer.

Uncle Myron said, "Well?"

"I have nothing else to report at this time."

"What does that mean?"

The groundskeeper, his face still white, started securing the casket with nylon belts.

"The casket will be at the medical examiner's office," he continued. "That is all I can tell you at this time."

Bow Tie moved to the cab of the pickup truck and slid into the passenger seat. The driver started up the engine. I hurried toward his window.

"When?" I asked.

"When what?"

"When will the medical examiner open the casket?"

He checked his clipboard again, but it seemed as if it were just for show, as if he already knew the answer.

"Now," he said.

CHAPTER 2

We were at the medical examiner's office, waiting for the casket to be opened, when my cell phone rang.

I was all set to ignore the call. The answer to the key question of my life—was my father dead or alive?—was mere moments away.

A phone call could wait, right?

Then again, I was just hanging around. Maybe a phone call would be a welcome distraction. I quickly checked the caller ID and saw it was my best friend Ema. Ema's real name is Emma, but she dresses all in black and has a bunch of tattoos, so some of the kids, way back when, considered her "emo" and then someone combined "Emma" with "emo" and cleverly (I'm being sarcastic when I say "cleverly") dubbed her Ema.

Still, the name stuck.

My first thought: Oh no, something bad happened to Spoon!

Uncle Myron leaned over my shoulder and pointed out the caller ID. "Is that Angelica Wyatt's daughter?"

I frowned. Like this was his business. "Yep."

"You two have become pretty tight."

I frowned some more. Like this was his business. "Yep."

I wasn't sure what to do here. I could step away from my hovering uncle and answer it. Uncle Myron could be pretty thick, but even he'd get the message. I held up the phone and said to him, "Uh, do you mind?"

"What? Oh, right. Sure. Sorry."

I hit the answer button and said, "Hey."

"Hey."

I mentioned that Ema was my best friend. We have only known each other a few weeks, but they've been dangerous and crazy weeks, life-affirming and life-threatening weeks. People could be friends a lifetime and not come close to the bond that had formed between us.

"Any word yet on the, uh . . . ?" Ema didn't know how to finish that sentence. Neither did I.

"It could come at any time," I said. "I'm at the medical examiner's office right now."

"Oh, sorry. I shouldn't have disturbed you."

There was something in her tone that I didn't like. I felt my heart leap into my throat.

"What's wrong?" I asked. "Is this about Spoon?"

Spoon was my second-best friend, I guess. Last time I saw him, he was lying in a hospital bed. He had been shot, saving our lives, and it was now possible that he'd never walk again. I blocked that horrible thought nonstop. I also dwelled on it nonstop.

"No," she said.

"Have you heard anything new?"

"No. His parents aren't letting me visit either."

Spoon's mom and dad had forbidden me from entering his room. They blamed me for what happened. Then again, so did I.

"So what's wrong?" I asked.

"Look, I shouldn't have called. It isn't a big deal. Really."

Which only made me sure that whatever it was, it was a big deal. Really.

I was about to argue and insist she tell me why she had called, but Bow Tie came back into the room.

"Gotta go," I said to her. "I'll call you when I can."

I hung up. Myron and I stepped toward Bow Tie. He had his head down, taking notes.

"Well?" Myron said.

"We should have the results in a few moments."

I realized that I had been holding my breath. I let it out now. Then I asked, "What was all that whispering about?"

"Pardon?"

"At the cemetery. With the guys digging and the one oper-ating the bulldozer."

"Oh," he said. "That."

I waited.

Bow Tie cleared his throat. "The groundskeepers"—so, okay, that's what they were called—"noted that the casket felt a little . . ." He looked up as though searching for the next word.

After three seconds that felt like an hour passed, I said, "Felt a little what?"

And then he said it: "Light."

Myron said, "As in weight?"

"Well, yes. But they were wrong."

That didn't make any sense. "They were wrong about the casket feeling light?"

"Yes."

"How?"

He lifted his clipboard, as if it could ward off attacks. "That is all I can say until I have the necessary paperwork."

"What necessary paperwork?"

"I have to go now."

"But—"

The door opened behind me. A woman in a business suit stepped into the room. We all slowly turned and stared at her.

"The medical examiner is finished."

"And?"

The woman looked left and then right, as though someone might be eavesdropping. "Please follow me," she said. "The medical examiner is ready to speak to you."

CHAPTER 3

"Thank you for your patience. I'm Dr. Botnick."

I expected the medical examiner to look ghoulish or creepy or something. Think about it. Medical examiners deal with dead people all day. They slice them open and try to figure out what killed them.

But Dr. Botnick was a tiny woman with an inappropriately happy smile and the kind of red hair that borders on orange. Her office had been completely stripped of any sort of personality. There was nothing personal in the entire room—no family photographs, for example, but then again, in a room filled with so much death, did people want to stare at images of her loved ones? Her desk was bare except for a brown leather desk pad with matching letter tray (empty), memo holder, pencil cup (two pens and one pencil), and a letter opener. The walls had diplomas, and nothing else.

She kept smiling at us. I looked at Myron. He looked lost.

"I'm sorry," she said. "I'm not very good with people. Then again, none of my patients complain." She started laughing. I didn't join in. Neither did Uncle Myron. She cleared her throat and said, "Get it?"

"Got it," I said.

"Because my patients, well, they're dead."

"Got it," I said again.

"Inappropriate, right? My bad. Truth? I'm a little nervous. This is an unusual situation."

I felt my pulse pick up speed.

Dr. Botnick looked over at Myron. "Who are you?"

"Myron Bolitar."

"So you'd be Brad Bolitar's brother?"

"Yes."

Her eyes found mine. "And you must be his son?"

"That's right," I said.

She wrote something down on a sheet of paper. "Could you tell me the cause of death?"

"Car accident," I said.

"I see." She jotted another note. "Usually when people request we exhume a body, it is because they wish to move burial grounds. That isn't the case here, is it?"

Myron and I both said no.

"Where is Kitty Hammer Bolitar?" Dr. Botnick asked.

Kitty Hammer Bolitar was my mother.

"She's not here," Myron said.

"Well, yes, I can see that. Where is she?"

"She's indisposed," Myron said.

Dr. Botnick frowned. "Like in the bathroom?"

"No."

"Kitty Hammer Bolitar is listed as the wife and thus the next of kin," Dr. Botnick continued. "Where is she? She should be part of this."

I finally said, "She's in a drug rehabilitation center in New Jersey."

Again she met my eye. I saw kindness there and maybe a little bit of pity. "There was a famous tennis player named Kitty Hammer. I saw her in the US Open when she was only fifteen years old."

A rock formed in my chest.

"That's not relevant," Myron snapped.

Yes, that was my mother. At one point Kitty Hammer Bolitar had a chance of being one of the greatest female tennis players of all time, up there with Billie Jean King and the Williams sisters. Then something happened that eventually ended her career: She got pregnant.

With me.

"You're right," Dr. Botnick said. "My apologies."

"Look," Uncle Myron said, "is his body in there or not?"

I watched her face for some kind of sign, but there was nothing. Dr. Botnick would have made a great poker player. She turned her attention to me. "Is that why you're here?"

"Yes," I said.

"To find out if your father is in the right casket?"

I said yes again.

"Why do you think your father wouldn't be in there?"

How could I possibly explain it?

Dr. Botnick looked at me as though she really wanted to help. But even in my own head it sounded insane. I couldn't tell her about the Bat Lady, who may be Lizzy Sobek, the Holocaust hero everyone thought had died in World War II. I couldn't tell her about the Abeona Shelter, the secret society that rescued children, and how Ema, Spoon, Rachel, and I had risked our lives in its service. I couldn't tell her about that creepy paramedic with the sandy hair and green eyes, the one who took my father away and then, eight months later, tried to kill me.

Who would believe such crazy talk?

Uncle Myron saw me squirm in my seat. "The reasons are confidential," he said, trying to come to my rescue. "Would you please just tell us what you found in the casket?"

Dr. Botnick started chewing on the end of her pen. We waited.

Finally, Myron tried again: "Is my brother in the casket, yes or no?"

She put the pen down on her desk and stood.

"Why don't you come with me and see for yourself?"

CHAPTER 4

We headed down the long corridor.

Dr. Botnick led the way. The corridor seemed to narrow as we walked, as though the tiled walls were closing in on us. I was about to move behind Myron, walking single file, when she stopped in front of a window.

"Wait here, please." Dr. Botnick poked her head in the door. "Ready?"

From inside, a voice said, "Give me two seconds."

Dr. Botnick closed the door. The window was thick. Wires crisscrossed inside of it, forming diamonds. There was a shade blocking our view.

"Are you ready?" Dr. Botnick asked.

I was shaking. We were here. This was it. I nodded. Myron said yes.

The shade rose slowly, like a curtain at a show. When it was all the way up—when I could see clearly into the room—it felt as though seashells had been pressed against my ears. For a moment, no one moved. No one spoke. We just stood there.

"What the—?"

The voice belonged to Uncle Myron. There, in front of us, was a gurney. And resting on the gurney was a silver urn.

Dr. Botnick put a hand on my shoulder. "Your father was cremated. His ashes were put in that urn and buried. It isn't customary, but it's not all that unusual either."

I shook my head.

Myron said, "Are you telling us that there were only ashes in that casket?"

"Yes."

"DNA," I said.

"Pardon?"

"Can you run a DNA test on the ashes?"

"I don't understand. Why would I do that?"

"To confirm that they belong to my father."

"To confirm . . . ?" Dr. Botnick shook her head. "That technology doesn't exist, I'm sorry."

I looked at Myron. There were tears in my eyes. "Don't you see?" I said.

"See what?"

"He's alive."

Myron's face turned white. In the corner of my eye I could see Bow Tie heading down the corridor toward us.

"Mickey . . . ," Myron began.

"Someone is covering their tracks," I insisted. "We wouldn't cremate him."

"I'm afraid that's not true."

It was Bow Tie. He held up a sheet of paper.

"What's that?" I asked.

"This is an authorization to have the body of Brad Bolitar cremated per the legal requirements for the State of California. It is all on the up-and-up, including the notarized signature of the next of kin."

Uncle Myron reached out for the sheet, but I grabbed it first. I scanned to the bottom of the page.

It had been signed by my mother.

I could feel Myron reading over my shoulder.

Kitty Hammer Bolitar had signed a lot of autographs during her tennis days. Her signature was fairly unique with the giant *K* and the curl on the right side of the *H*. This signature had both.

"It's a forgery!" I shouted, though it didn't look like a forgery at all. "This has to be a fake."

They all stared at me as though an arm had suddenly sprouted out of the middle of my forehead.

"It was notarized," Bow Tie said. "That means an independent person witnessed and confirmed that your mother signed it."

I shook my head. "You don't understand . . ."

Bow Tie took the sheet back from me. "I'm sorry," he said. "There is nothing more we can do for you."

CHAPTER 5

Dead end.

We sat in the airport and waited to board our flight home. Uncle Myron frowned at his smartphone, concentrating a little too hard on the screen. "Mickey?"

I looked at him.

"Don't you think it's time you told me what's going on?"

It was. Uncle Myron deserved to know. He had called in favors and put himself on the line. He had, in a sense, earned my trust. But there were other things to consider. First of all, I had been warned more than once by those in Abeona Shelter *not* to tell Myron. I couldn't just ignore that advice.

Second—and this was always front and center—I still blamed Myron for what happened to my parents. When my mother got pregnant with me, Uncle Myron reacted badly to the news. He didn't trust my mother. He and my dad fought over it. My parents ended up running away overseas and then coming back years later and then . . . well, then it led to my dad being "maybe dead" and my mother being locked up in a drug rehabilitation center.

Uncle Myron waited for my answer. I was wondering how to tell him no when I remembered that I still needed to call Ema back. I held up the phone and said, "I have to take this," even though the phone hadn't rung.

I moved away from the gate and hit Ema on my speed dial. She answered immediately.

"So?" Ema said.

"So nothing."

"Huh? I thought they were about to open the casket."

"They were. I mean, they did."

I explained about the cremation. She listened, as always, without interrupting. Ema was one of those people who listened with everything they had. She focused on your face. Her eyes didn't dart to all corners. She didn't nod at inappropriate times. Even now, even when she was just on the phone with me, I could feel that concentration.

"And you're sure it's her signature?"

"It certainly looks like it."

"But it could be forged," Ema said.

"Doubtful. I mean, there was a notary who witnessed it or something. But it could be . . ." My words trailed off.

"What?"

"After my father died, well, that was when she fell apart."

"She started taking drugs?"

"Yes," I said, remembering it all now. "In fact, Mom was so out of it . . . I don't know how she could have made a decision like that."

"So what now?"

"I fly home. I have basketball practice."

I know what you're thinking. Who cares about basketball practice at a time like this? Answer: I do. I get that that sounds warped. But even now—or maybe especially now—I needed to be back on the court. I needed basketball to be a priority. It was the place I thrived and escaped, and no matter what, I longed for it.

"Anything new on Spoon's condition?" I asked.

"No."

"How about Rachel?"

Silence.

I waited. Asking about Rachel may have been a mistake, I don't know. Rachel was a part of our group, much as she, being immensely popular and probably the hottest girl in the school, seemed to have nothing in common with us.

"Rachel's fine," Ema said, her voice like a door slamming shut. "She's dealing, I guess."

I needed to reach out to Rachel when I got back. I had dropped a huge bomb on her—a life-altering bomb—and then I had flown away to Los Angeles. I needed to remedy that.

"So why did you call before?" I asked.

"It can wait till you get home."

"Talk to me, Ema. I need the distraction."

She took a deep breath. I could see her now, sitting alone in that huge gated mansion. "Why us?" she asked.

I knew what she meant. Nothing here had been accidental. A secret group called the Abeona Shelter had somehow recruited us—Ema, Spoon, Rachel, me—to help them rescue children and teens. This was never stated. We never applied for the job, and it wasn't as though they had come to us. It just sort of . . . happened.

"I ask myself that every day," I said.

"And?"

"I don't know."

"There has to be a reason," Ema said. "First Ashley, then Rachel, and now—"

"Now what?"

"Someone else is missing," she said.

My grip on the phone tightened. "Who?"

"You don't know him."

Silly, but I had thought that I knew everyone Ema knew. Maybe it was because she always played the big-girl-outcast-loner to perfection. The other kids made fun of her weight and her all-black clothes. Ema always sat by herself at lunch in the cafeteria. She had taken sullen and raised it to an art form.

"But you do?" I said.

"Yes."

"Who?"

"He's . . . well, he's kind of my boyfriend."

CHAPTER 6

Man, I hadn't expected that answer.

How could I not know Ema had a boyfriend? How could she keep something like that from me? I mean, don't get me wrong. I thought it was great. Ema was so awesome. She deserved somebody.

So why was I annoyed?

Because we told each other everything, didn't we? Now I wasn't so sure. *I* told her everything, but maybe it was just a one-way street. Clearly Ema hadn't been equally forthcoming.

How could she not tell me that she had a freakin' boyfriend?

Then again, had I told her about Rachel and me, about how there just might be something more between us?

No.

Why not? If Ema was just my friend—if it didn't matter that she was a girl or whatever—why wouldn't I tell her about Rachel?

"You okay?" Uncle Myron asked.

We were on the plane now, crammed next to each other in the last row. We are both tall, and the legroom in coach is designed for someone about two feet shorter.

"I'm fine," I said.

"So now what?" Uncle Myron asked.

"What do you mean?"

"You asked me to help get your father's grave exhumed, right?"

"Right."

Uncle Myron tried to shrug, but the seat was too small for it. "So now that we've done that, what's your next step?"

I had wondered that myself, of course. "I don't know yet."

As soon as we landed, I called Ema. No answer. I tried Rachel's phone. No answer. I texted them both that I was back in New Jersey. I placed a call to the hospital again, trying to get through to Spoon's room, but the operator wouldn't patch the call through.

"No calls allowed to that room," the operator explained.

I didn't like that.

We had landed on time, which meant that I could still make basketball practice. I had missed the past few days because of this trip. That would set me back with the team, and it worried me a little. I hadn't actually practiced with the varsity, and I knew that I would be way behind.

Kasselton High, my new school, has a varsity and junior

varsity team. The varsity is for juniors and seniors. Freshmen and sophomores play JV, and so far, in Coach Grady's dozen years of coaching the Kasselton Camels, he has never had a freshman or sophomore on the varsity.

Humble-brag alert: I, a lowly sophomore, have been invited to try out for the varsity team.

I couldn't wait to get on the court, but as Uncle Myron pulled his car to a stop in front of the school, I felt the butterflies start flying around my stomach. Myron must have seen the look on my face.

"You nervous?"

"What, me?" I shook my head firmly. "No."

Uncle Myron put his hand on my shoulder. "It may take a while to warm up after a long flight," he went on, "but once you get on the court and the ball is in your hand—"

"Right, thanks," I said, not really wanting to hear it.

It wasn't worrying about my performance that stirred those butterflies.

It was my teammates. In short, they all hated me.

None of the seniors and juniors liked the idea of a lowly sophomore crashing their party.

I could hear laughter coming from the locker room, but as soon as I pushed open the door, all sound stopped as though someone had flicked a switch. Troy Taylor, the senior captain, glared at me. To put it mildly, Troy and I had issues. I looked away and opened a locker.

"Not there," Troy said.

"What?"

"This row is for lettermen."

Everybody else was in this row. I looked at the other guys. Some had their heads lowered, tying their shoes too carefully. Some glared with open hostility. I looked for Buck, Troy's best friend and a total jerk, but he wasn't there.

I waited for someone to stick up for me or, at least, comment. No one did. Troy smirked and made a shooing gesture in my direction with his hand. My face reddened in embarrassment. I wondered what I should do, whether I should fight or back down.

Not worth it, I decided.

I hated giving Troy the satisfaction, but I remembered something my father told me: Don't win the battle and lose the war.

I took my stuff, moved into the next row, and changed into shorts and a reversible practice jersey. After I laced up my sneakers, I headed out to the gym. That sweet echo of dribbling basketballs calmed me a bit, but as soon as I opened the door, all dribbling stopped.

Oh, grow up.

There were four or five guys at each of three baskets. Troy shot at the one on the far right. His glare was already in place. I looked again for Buck—he was always with Troy, always following Troy's lead—but he wasn't here. I wondered whether Buck had gotten injured and, cruel as it sounded, I really hoped that was the case.

I looked toward the guys standing around the basket in the middle. If those faces were windows, they were all slammed shut with shades lowered. At the third basket, I spotted Brandon Foley, the team center and other captain. Brandon was the tallest kid on the team, six foot eight, and in the past, he had been the only one to acknowledge my existence. As I stepped toward him, he met my eye and gave his head a small shake.

Terrific.

The heck with it. I moved over to a basket in the far left corner and shot alone. My face burned. I let the burn sink deep inside of me. The burn was good. The burn would fuel my game and make me better. The burn would let me forget, for a few moments anyway, that I still didn't know what really happened to my father. The burn would let me forget—no, not really—that my friend Spoon was in the hospital and may never walk again and that it was all my fault.

Maybe that explained why all my potential teammates, even Brandon Foley, had turned on me. Maybe they too blamed me for what happened to the nerd that they all enjoyed bullying.

It didn't matter. Shoot, get the rebound, shoot. Stare at the rim, only the rim; never watch the ball in flight; feel the grooves on your fingertips. Shoot, *swish,* shoot, *swish.* Let the rest of the world fade away for a little while.

Do you have something like this in your life? Something you do or play that makes the entire world, at least for a little while, fade away? That was how basketball was. I could sometimes focus so hard that everything else ceased to exist. There was the ball. There was the hoop. Nothing else.

"Hey, hotshot."

The sound of Troy's voice knocked me out of my stupor. I looked around. The gym was empty.

"Team meeting for non-lettermen," Troy said. "Room one seventy-eight. Hurry."

"Where is that?"

Troy frowned. "You serious?"

"I'm new to the school, remember?"

"Lower level. Push through the metal doors. Hurry. Coach Grady hates when someone shows up late."

"Thanks."

I dropped the ball and hustled down the corridor. As I took the stairs down, a small niggling started at the back of my brain. It wondered how come Coach Grady would call a meeting so far from the gym. I wish that I had stopped there and listened to that niggling. But there was really no time. And what was I going to do anyway, run back upstairs and ask my buddy Troy for more details on the meeting?

So I ran down the corridor. There was no else in the halls. The echo of my sneakers slapping the linoleum sounded as loud as . . .

. . . as gunshots.

My head started spinning. Where exactly was I? The lower level was for senior classes. I had never been here before. But if my sense of direction was correct, I was pretty close to being right on top of where Spoon had been shot just a few days earlier.

I hurried my step.

Room 166. Then room 168. I was getting closer. 170, 172 . . .

Up ahead I saw the metal doors Troy had mentioned. I pushed through them. They closed behind me with a bang.

And locked me out.

I stopped and closed my eyes. There was no room 178. Practice was probably starting right now. I would have to go out the back, through the football field, and around to the front entrance in order to make my way to the gym.

I ran as fast as I could but it still took me nearly ten minutes to get back. My teammates were already doing the weave drill when I burst in through the door. Coach Grady was not pleased. He turned and snapped, "You're late, Bolitar."

"It isn't my . . ."

I stopped. What exactly was I going to say here? Troy looked at me with that same stupid smirk. He knew. I had two choices. One, tell Coach Grady what really happened, in which case Coach Grady might or might not believe me, but either way I'd be forever labeled a tattletale. Or, two, keep my mouth shut.

"Sorry, Coach."

But Coach Grady wasn't done. "Being late to practice is disrespectful to both your teammates and your coaches."

I nodded. "It won't happen again."

"You haven't even made the team yet."

"Yes, sir."

"And this won't help your cause."

"I understand, sir. I'm really sorry."

Coach Grady stared at me a beat too long. "Run three laps and then get on line. Troy?"

"Yes, Coach?"

"Where's Buck?"

I would say that Buck was meaner than a snake, but that wouldn't be nice to the snake.

"I don't know, Coach. He didn't pick up his cell."

"Odd. He's never missed a practice before. Okay, five-second-denial drill. Get into it."

Practice didn't get much better. Whenever we were working on plays, the guys would throw it at my feet, making it nearly impossible to catch. When we scrimmaged, they froze me out, never passing me the ball no matter how open I was. Of course, I got my share of rebounds. I scored twice off steals. But still. If your teammates freeze you out, there is only so much you can do.

And then, with just a minute left in practice, I saw a glorious opening.

I was covering Brandon Foley. He grabbed a rebound and threw a long outlet pass to Troy Taylor. Troy had been what we call "basket-hanging"—not playing defense and staying close to his own basket for easy points. Troy caught the ball and slowed down his dribble. He was taking his time, preparing for takeoff, revving himself up for a big-time slam dunk.

The other guys hung back, watching, waiting to see whether Troy threw it down with one hand or two, or whether he tried a reverse dunk or something trickier.

I didn't.

I sprinted toward the basket with everything I had. Up ahead of me, Troy took off into the air. His hand was above the rim, palming the ball. He was maybe half a second away from dunking the ball through the hoop when I leapt up from behind him and swatted the ball away.

"What the—?" Troy shouted in surprise.

A completely clean block.

"Foul!" he yelled.

I said nothing, just jogged toward the bouncing ball.

"You fouled me!"

I picked up the ball. I had knocked it out of bounds. It was his team's possession. My father had taught me that you let your game do the talking. You don't yell at referees. You don't trash-talk. You just play.

I handed Troy the ball. He snatched it away.

"He fouled me!" Troy shouted again.

"Take the ball out of bounds, Troy," Coach Grady said. "Run the stack."

"But—"

"It's just a scrimmage. Let's go. Ten seconds left."

Troy didn't like it. He muttered something under his breath.

I ignored him and got ready. I covered Brandon Foley tightly. I knew that he was the first option on the stack. Troy would want to lob it over my head to Brandon. I wouldn't let that happen.

Troy yelled, "Break!" and all the players started to move. I kept a forearm on Brandon, trying to time his jump. I had my back to the ball, my eyes on my man, guarding him closely.

Seconds ticked by.

If five seconds passed, we got the ball. It was getting pretty close to that. I sneaked a glance to see what Troy was about to do.

But he'd been waiting for me to do just that.

When I spotted the grin on Troy's face, I knew that I had made yet another mistake. Troy had been hoping that curiosity would get the better of me. Without warning or hesitation, Troy whipped the ball right at my face.

There was no time to react. The ball landed hard against my nose like a giant fist. I staggered back. I saw stars. My eyes started to water. My head felt numb. I tried to stay standing, tried like hell not to give Troy the satisfaction of going down, but I couldn't remain upright.

I dropped to one knee and cupped my nose in both hands. Brandon put a hand on my shoulder. "You okay?"

Coach Grady blew the whistle. "What the heck was that?"

"Hey, I'm sorry," Troy said, all nice and innocent. "I was trying to get the ball to Brandon."

I shook Brandon's hand off my shoulder. The pain was

subsiding. The nose wasn't broken. I stood as quickly as I could. My head reeled in protest, but I didn't back down.

I blinked away the tears and met Troy's eye. "Whose ball is it?" I asked in as calm a voice as I could muster.

Brandon said, "You sure you're—"

"Off you," Troy said. "It hit your face and went out of bounds."

"Then your ball," I said. "Let's play."

But right then, Coach Stashower, the assistant coach, hurried back into the gymnasium. He whispered something into Coach Grady's ear. Coach Grady's face lost color.

"Okay, that's it," Coach Grady said. "Practice is over. Take a lap and shower up."

I took the lap quickly and headed into my solo locker row. I grabbed my cell phone and checked the messages. Only one text—it was from Ema: **coming over after practice? let me know time.**

I quickly typed that practice had just ended and, yes, of course I'd be over.

After all, we had to find her missing "boyfriend."

There was still nothing from Rachel. I didn't know what to do about it. I was sure some "helpful" adult would say something like "give it time," but I hated that advice. I had blown it. Uncle Myron had warned me that even the ugliest truth was better than the prettiest of lies. I had listened to that advice. I had told Rachel the ugly truth about her mother's death.

Now, it seemed, she didn't want to see me again.

I thought about that. I thought about Spoon in that hospital bed. I thought about the ashes in my father's grave. I thought about my mother in rehab. I thought about basketball, about my dreams of finally playing on a real team and how, now that it had come true, all my teammates hated me.

I sat by my locker. Sweat dripped off me. I could hear my teammates making jokes and enjoying that easy, laughing friendship I had never really known. Emotionally drained, I stayed where I was. I decided that I'd wait it out. I'd let the rest of the team shower and get dressed, and then when everyone was gone, I'd get ready.

I just didn't have the strength to face them any more today.

Troy was in the middle of some long-winded story when Assistant Coach Stashower stuck his head in the door. "Troy? Coach wants to see you in his office."

"I'm just finishing up a joke—"

"Now, Troy."

Everyone made a friendly mocking "oooo" sound as Troy headed out. Then the rest of the guys showered and got dressed. I pretended to check my iPhone for important messages. Ten minutes passed. The guys started to file out with back slaps, figuring out who would ride in whose car, figuring a time to meet up at the Heritage Diner and then hang out at whose house.

I'd thought that the entire team had left when Brandon

Foley came around the corner and sat on the bench next to my locker.

"Tough practice," Brandon said.

I shrugged. "No big deal."

"Troy isn't really such a bad guy."

"Yeah," I said, "he's a real prince."

Brandon smiled at that one. I knew that Brandon Foley was one of the most popular kids in the school. He was president of the student council, president of the Key Club, president of the local chapter of the National Honor Society, and as I mentioned before, co-captain (with Troy) of the basketball team.

You know the type. Good guy, but he wants everyone to like him.

"You need to understand the situation," Brandon said.

"Uh-huh," I said.

"It's mild hazing," Brandon said. "You're the only sophomore."

It was a lot more than mild hazing, but I didn't see much point in continuing with this conversation.

"Mickey?"

"What?"

"You know that this team won the county championship last year, right?"

"Yes," I said.

"And that we were within one game of winning the states," Brandon continued. "Do you know how long it's been since Kasselton High actually won it?"

I did. The big win was memorialized all over the walls of the gym in the form of banners and retired jerseys. Twenty-five years ago, Uncle Myron, the school's all-time leading scorer and rebounder, led the Kasselton Camels to their only state championship. One of his teammates—the *second* leading scorer and *second* leading rebounder on that team—was none other than Edward Taylor, Troy's father. He was now the town sheriff.

Bad blood across two generations.

"What's your point?" I said.

"The point is, last year our team started five juniors, so we're all back. The five of us have all played together since we were Biddy All-Stars in fifth grade. Troy, Buck, Alec, Damien, and me—we grew up together. We've been the starting five since we were eleven years old. This may not seem like a big deal to you."

But it did seem like a big deal. I never had anything like that. My parents had lived overseas my entire life. We jumped from place to place, country to country, mostly in the Third World. We lived the life of nomads, backpacking, setting up tents, living in small villages. I had no idea what it was like to have friends like that. As I said before, Ema and Spoon were my best friends ever, and I had only known them a few weeks.

"So now," Brandon said, in his calm, rational, mature voice, "the five of us are seniors. This will be our last year together. We will go off to college and never be on the same team again. We've been waiting for this moment pretty much our whole lives. And now, because of you, one of us won't be a starter anymore."

"You don't know—"

Brandon held up a hand. "Please, Mickey, let's not play humble. You know how good you are. I know how good you are. Troy has always been our leading scorer and best player. Soon it will be you. So he knows it too. You've been at this school, what, a few weeks. In that time, you've taken his girlfriend and soon you'll have his spot on the team."

He was talking about Rachel. I wanted to correct him—I hadn't taken her away and she wasn't my girlfriend—but maybe it was better to just stay quiet.

Brandon stood. "Give him time to get used to that, okay?"

"I didn't steal his girlfriend," I said.

So much for staying quiet.

"What?"

"Rachel broke it off with him before I ever got here."

"That's not the point."

"Of course it is. And I can't help it if I'm a better player than he is."

"I didn't say you could," Brandon replied. "I'm just letting you know what's going on."

"I don't care," I said.

"Excuse me?"

"Troy is a jerk. You're justifying his bullying behavior—not just of me, but of Ema and Spoon too. He's been on my case since day one—before he ever saw me take a shot—and he just intentionally whipped a basketball at my face. So, sorry, Brandon, I'm not really in the mood to hear someone excuse his bullying."

"I'm not excusing it."

I stood up. "Yeah, you are. And you let it happen. You, the big co-captain and president of everything in this stupid school, just stood there today and let it happen."

Brandon didn't like that. "Look, Mickey, I came over here to help you."

"You're a little late, Brandon. And if your help is to justify why your old best friend hates me, I'm good, thanks. He's the one you should be talking to, not me."

Brandon looked down at me another moment or two. I wanted to take it back. He had been the only one to reach out a hand in friendship, and I had slapped it away. But I was also angry and tired and jet-lagged and just sick of all the crap that kept piling on me. I didn't want to hear about Troy's problems. I had enough on my own.

Still, I ended up saying, "Brandon, I didn't mean—"

"See you around."

He turned and left without another word.

Fine.

I really had nothing to say to him anyway. I was finally alone. I got undressed and headed into the shower. Have you ever been alone in a locker room? Every sound echoes like it's been miked up. I turned on the water and stepped under the wonderfully harsh spray. I took my time, letting the water pound on my back and head, closing my eyes and breathing deeply.

Calm down, I told myself.

I had just gotten out of the shower when I heard the locker room door burst open. I peeked around the corner.

It was Troy.

He didn't see me. I stayed where I was. He collapsed onto the bench in front of his locker. His face fell into his hands. I heard a sound, a sound like . . .

Troy was crying!

For a moment I thought that maybe Coach Grady had bawled him out for his behavior today. Maybe Coach had seen how Troy had punked me with that fake meeting and whipped the ball into my face, and that was why he had called him into his office.

But I would soon learn that this had nothing to do with me.

The locker room door opened up again. It was Coach Stashower.

"You got your things, Troy?"

Troy sniffled and wiped the tears off his face with his forearm. "It's a lie, you know."

"We heard you."

"I'm being set up."

"Either way, I'm supposed to stay with you while you clean out your locker."

"Now?"

"Now, Troy. It all has to go."

Troy looked as though he was about to protest and then thought better of it. He opened his locker. He took out his bag and angrily stuffed everything into it. Everything. Sneakers, clothes, loose change. His shampoo. His cologne (cologne?). Even, ugh, an old photograph of Troy with his arm around Rachel in her cheerleading uniform that he'd taped to the inside of the locker door.

He jammed it all into his gym bag.

What the heck was going on?

"I'll escort you out," Coach Stashower said in a firm voice when Troy was done.

"No need," Troy said. He stormed toward the door and flung it open. "It's a lie. All of it."

Then Troy was gone.

CHAPTER 7

I should have felt elated. My big enemy was apparently off the team. But I didn't. I felt confused and a little lost. Then again, that seemed to be my permanent status lately. I was at my best when I didn't have to think too much—either when I was on the court or when I had a specific task.

So what was my next task?

Help Ema find her missing boyfriend, I guess.

I walked up the long driveway and crossed the expansive front grounds. I'd barely put my fingertip on the doorbell in front of Ema's enormous mansion when the door swung slowly open.

"Master Mickey. Welcome."

It was Niles, the family butler, speaking with an accent so pronounced, it had to be fake. He wore a tuxedo or tails or something like that. His posture was ramrod straight. He arched one eyebrow.

Ema ran to the door. "Cut that out, Niles."

"Sorry, madam."

Ema rolled her eyes. "He's been watching a lot of British television."

"Oh," I said, though I wasn't sure I got it.

It was funny watching the two of them standing there. Both wore black, but that was where the similarities ended. Niles wore formal wear. Ema was in full goth mode—black clothes, jet-black hair, black lipstick, white makeup. She had silver studs going all the way up her ears, a pierced eyebrow, and one skull ring on each hand.

As we headed down the stairs, I couldn't help but stare at the movie posters. They all featured films starring the gorgeous Angelica Wyatt. Some were headshots. Some were full body. Sometimes she was alone. Sometimes she was with some guy. On the bottom step, there was one for that romantic comedy she did with Matt Damon last year.

Only a handful of people knew that Angelica Wyatt—yes, *the* Angelica Wyatt—was Ema's mom.

"So tell me what happened in California," Ema said.

We sat on oversize beanbag chairs. I told her everything. When I was done, Ema said, "Maybe it was your father's wish."

"What? Being cremated?"

"Right, a lot of people choose that," Ema said. "It's a possibility, right?"

I thought about it. We had traveled all over the world. Most foreign cultures—most cultures my father admired—preferred cremation to burial. I remembered that my father once bemoaned the "waste" of good land, land that could have been used to grow crops, because it was being used as a graveyard.

Could he have told Mom he wanted to be cremated?

I thought some more. Then I said, "No."

"You're sure?"

"If Dad had wanted to be cremated, he wouldn't then want to be buried too. He'd choose one or the other."

Ema nodded. "But it was your mother's signature on the form?"

"Yes."

"So?"

"So I need to ask her about it. The problem is, she's not allowed visitors in rehab right now. She's going through withdrawal."

"How much longer?"

"I don't know." I looked at Ema. Yes, she was interested, but I knew what she was doing. For some reason, she was asking all these questions to stall. "So tell me about your missing boyfriend."

"Before I do," Ema said, "I wanted to show you something."

"Okay."

She started pulling up her shirt.

"Uh," I said, because I'm good with words.

"Relax, perv. I want to show you a tattoo."

"Uh," I said again.

"You'll see why."

Ema was loaded up with tattoos. This helped cultivate her bad-girl image. She wore them almost like a fence, warning people to stay back. Yes, I know a lot of people have tattoos, but Ema was only a high school freshman. Many of the kids were intimidated that a girl so young could have so many. How did she get her parents' permission?

I had wondered that myself.

But more recently I learned the simple truth: The tattoos were temporary. She had a friend named Agent at a tattoo parlor called Tattoos While U Wait. Agent liked to try out designs before putting them on someone in a permanent way. He used Ema's skin as a practice canvas.

Ema turned her back to me. "Look."

There, in the center of her back, was a familiar image to Ema, Spoon, Rachel, and me.

A butterfly. More specifically, the Tisiphone *Abeona* butterfly.

That image haunted us. I had seen it on a grave behind Bat Lady's house. I had seen it on Rachel's hospital room door. I had seen it in an old picture of hippies from the sixties. I had even seen the image of that butterfly in an old photograph of the famous Lizzy Sobek, the young girl who led children to safety during the Holocaust. I saw it atop my father's "maybe" grave, on the back of a photograph in Bat Lady's basement, even in a tattoo parlor.

"You told me about that," I said.

"I know. But I went back to have it redone. You know. Have Agent make it bright or change it. The tattoos usually wear off after a few weeks."

I felt a small chill ripple across my back. "But?"

"But he couldn't."

I knew the answer but I asked anyway. "Why?"

"It's permanent," Ema said. "Agent said he doesn't know how that happened. But the butterfly is there. For good."

I said nothing.

"What's going on, Mickey?"

"I don't know."

We sat there in silence. I finally broke it. "Tell me about your missing boyfriend."

For a second or two, she didn't move. She swallowed, blinked a few times, and then stared at the floor. "*Boyfriend* may be putting it a little too strongly."

I waited.

"Mickey?"

"What?"

Ema started twisting the skull ring on her right hand. "You have to promise me something."

Her body language was all wrong. Ema was about confidence. She was big and confident and didn't care who noticed.

She was comfortable in her own skin. Now, all of a sudden, that confidence was gone.

"Okay," I said.

"You have to promise you won't make fun of me."

"Are you serious?"

She just looked at me.

"Okay, okay, I promise. It's odd, that's all."

"What's odd?" she asked.

"This promise. I thought you didn't care what people think of you."

"I don't," Ema said. "I care what *you* think of me."

A second passed. Then another. Then I said, "Oh," because I'm really, really good with words. It was, of course, a dumb comment on my part—the stuff about her not caring. Everyone cares what people think. Some just hide it better.

"So tell me," I said.

"I met a guy in a chat room," Ema said.

I blinked once. Then I said, "You hang out in chat rooms?"

"You promised."

"I'm not making fun."

"You're judging," she said. "That's just as bad."

"I'm not. I'm just surprised, that's all."

"It's not like you think," Ema said. "See, I've been helping my mom with her social networking. She's clueless. So is her manager and her agent and her personal assistant—whatever. So I set some promotional stuff up for her—Twitter, Facebook, you know the deal. And now I watch it for her."

"Okay," I said.

"Anyway, in this chat room, I met this guy."

I just looked at her.

"What?" she said.

"Nothing."

"You're judging again."

"I'm just sitting here," I said, spreading my hands. "If you see something more on my face, that's more about you than me."

"Right, sure."

"I'm just surprised, okay? What kind of chat room was this anyway?"

"It's for Angelica Wyatt fans."

I tried sooo hard to keep my face expressionless.

"There you go again!" she shouted.

"Stop looking at my face and tell me what happened. You're in an Angelica Wyatt chat room. You start talking to a guy. Am I right so far?"

Ema looked sheepish. "Yeah."

"Are you using an alias?"

"No."

"Why not?"

"Why would I? No one knows I'm Angelica Wyatt's daughter."

Not even me until I followed her from school last week. In school, Ema was the subject of much speculation. Every school, I'm told, has that one kid who seems to come out of the woods to school every day. No one knows where he or

she lives. No one has been to his or her house. Rumors start—
as they did about Ema. She lived in a cabin in the woods,
some speculated. Her father abused her maybe. He sold drugs.
Something.

Ema actually encouraged those rumors to hide the truth:
She was the daughter of a world-famous movie star.

"I use my own name in the chat room," Ema said, "so I can
be just another fan."

"Okay, go on."

"So anyway, I started chatting with this guy. Then we
started e-mailing and texting, that kind of thing." Her face
turned red. "He told me about his life. He told me he used to
live in Europe but they had moved to the United States last
year. We talked about books and movies and feelings. It . . . it
got pretty intimate."

My face twisted into a grimace.

"Ew, gross," Ema snapped. "Not that kind of intimate!"

"I didn't say—"

"Stop, okay? And never play poker, Mickey. You'd be terrible at it. I mean, we *talked*. We really talked and opened up.
At first, okay, I figured that maybe this guy was a fake, you
know? Like I was being played."

"A prank," I said. "Catfished."

"Right. I mean, you know me. I don't trust easily. But as
time went on . . ." Ema's eyes lit up. "It was weird, but we
both changed. Especially him. He might have started out playing some kind of game, but he became real. I can't explain it."

I nodded, trying to move her along. "So you two got close."

"Yes."

"You felt like he was starting to open up to you."

"Yes. A few days ago, he said that he had something really important to tell me. That he had to confess something. I figured, uh-oh, here we go. He's really an eleven-year-old girl or he's married and thirty-eight. Something like that."

"But that wasn't it?"

Ema shook her head. "No."

"So what was his big secret?"

"He ended up saying, forget it, it's no big deal," Ema said. She slid a little closer to me. "Don't you see? He chickened out. I can't explain this well. I'm summing up hundreds of texts and conversations. It was like something scared him from telling me the truth."

"You're right," I said.

"I am?"

I nodded. "You're not explaining this well."

Ema punched me in the arm. "Just listen, okay?"

"Okay."

"Jared and I finally set up a meet."

"Jared? His name is Jared?"

"Oh, now you're going to make fun of his name?"

I held up both hands.

"He lives in Connecticut. About two hours from here. So we agreed to meet at the Kasselton Mall. Jared had just gotten his license and could drive down. He said that he had to tell me something really important, something he could only tell me in person. He said that once we met, I'd understand everything."

"Understand everything about what?"

"About him. About us."

I was lost, but I just said, "Okay. So then what?"

"Then . . ." Ema stopped, shrugged. "Nothing."

"What do you mean, nothing?"

"What do you think I mean?" she snapped. "That's it. I went to the Kasselton Mall. I waited exactly where we said we'd meet—in that back corner of Ruby Tuesday's. But he never showed. I waited one hour. Then two. Then . . . all day, okay? I sat there all day."

"Jared never showed?"

"You got it."

"So what did you do then?" I asked.

"I texted him. But he didn't answer. I e-mailed him. Same thing. I went into our chat room, but he didn't come back. I even checked his Facebook page, but there was nothing there. It was like he had suddenly vanished into thin air."

Ema typed something onto her laptop and then turned it to me. It was a Facebook profile for a boy named Jared Lowell. I took one look at his profile picture and without thinking said, "You were catfished."

"What?"

The guy in the profile picture was ridiculously good-looking.

I don't mean everyday-high-school-quarterback good-looking. I mean TV-hunk, fronting-a-hot-boy-band good-looking.

"Forget it," I said.

Ema was angry now. "Why did you say that?"

"Forget it, okay?"

"No, why did you say that I was catfished when you saw his picture? It's because he's cute, right?"

"What? No." But my words sounded weak even in my own ears.

"You don't think a guy who looks like that could ever go for a girl who looks like me, right?"

"That's not it at all," I sorta-lied.

"If I were Rachel Caldwell, you'd have no trouble believing it—"

"It isn't that, Ema. But, I mean, look at him. Come on. If I told you I was having an online relationship with a girl I met in a chat room and, when you saw her picture, she looked like a famous swimsuit model, what would you think?"

"I'd believe you," she said. But now it was her voice that sounded weak.

"Right," I said. "Sure. And then when I was supposed to meet Miss Swimsuit Model in person, she suddenly vanished—would you still believe it?"

"Yes," she said a little too firmly.

I put my hands on her shoulders. "You're my best friend, Ema. You're the best friend I've ever had."

She looked down, her face reddening in embarrassment.

"I could lie to you and tell you that this all sounds on the up-and-up," I said. "But what kind of friend does that? I'm not saying your relationship with Jared isn't real. But if I don't have the courage to tell you how it looks, who will?"

That stopped her. Ema kept her face down. "So you think, what, it's a prank?"

"Maybe," I said. "That's all. Maybe it's just a joke."

She looked up at me. "A joke?"

"A cruel one, but yeah, maybe."

"Well, ha-ha." Ema shook her head. "Mickey, think about it. Let's say it was a prank. Let's say it was the mean kids in school. Like Troy or Buck, right? Let's say they set this whole thing up."

I waited.

Ema spread her arms. "Where's the payoff?"

I had no answer to that.

"They would have let me know, right? They would have mocked me. They would have rubbed it in my face or put the intimate conversations online. They'd let the world know what a fool I was, wouldn't they?"

A tear slid down her cheek.

"Why would Jared the prankster just vanish without having the last word?"

I swallowed. "I don't know," I said.

"Mickey?"

"What?"

"It is easy to make fun of these relationships. I used to do it too. But think about it. When it is just in writing like this, when it is just texts or e-mails, just your words and nothing else, it is actually more real. It doesn't matter what you look like or what table you sit at during lunch. It doesn't matter if you play quarterback or head up the chess club. All of that becomes irrelevant. It is just the two of you and your intelligence and your feelings. Do you see?"

"I guess," I admitted.

"Listen to me, Mickey. Look at my eyes and really listen."

I did. I looked into those eyes, and for a moment, I felt happily lost. I trusted those eyes. I believed in them.

"I know," Ema said. "Don't ask me how. But I know. We have to do this—even if you think I'm crazy."

"Why?"

"Because it's not up to us," Ema said.

"Huh? Of course it is."

Ema shook her head. "These things come to us, Mickey. It's bigger than we are."

"What do you mean?"

"You know what I mean."

"What, you think this is Abeona?"

She moved closer to me so we could share the laptop. I smelled her perfume. It was something new, something different. I had smelled it before, but couldn't place it. She pulled up

Jared's page again. "There has only been one new photograph added since Jared disappeared . . ."

When I saw the screen, I nearly gasped out loud.

There, on Jared Lowell's page, was a photograph of a butterfly.

Again, to be more specific, the Tisiphone Abeona.

"We have no choice," Ema said. "We need to find him."

We sat there for another moment, staring at that butterfly. I smelled her perfume again and felt a small rush. I looked at her. She looked at me. Our eyes met. Nothing was said. Nothing needed to be said.

And then my cell phone rang.

Our eye contact broke as though it were a dry twig. Ema looked away. I looked toward the caller ID on my phone. The number was blocked.

"Hello?"

An adult male said, "Is this Mickey Bolitar?"

The voice was grave and serious and maybe there was a small quake of fear in it.

"Yes, this is he," I said.

"This is Mr. Spindel, Arthur's father."

It took me a second to place the name, but when I did, I felt my pulse quicken. I always called Arthur Spindel "Spoon." His father, the man on the phone, was the head custodian at Kasselton High School—and Spoon's father.

"Is Spoon okay?" I said quickly.

Mr. Spindel didn't answer that directly. "Do you know where Emma Beaumont is?"

Emma was Ema. "She's right next to me."

"Could you please both come to the hospital?"

"Of course. When?"

"As soon as possible," Mr. Spindel said, and then he hung up.

CHAPTER 8

Niles drove us to Saint Barnabas Medical Center. He dropped us off at the front door. We sprinted to the reception desk in the lobby.

"Fifth floor," the receptionist said to us. "The elevator is on your right. Look for the signs for the ICU."

ICU. Spoon was still in the Intensive Care Unit. I felt my eyes well up, but I forced the tears back down.

We hurried to the elevator. I pressed the button repeatedly, as if that would somehow tell the elevator that we were in a rush. It took too long to arrive. We leapt in and of course three other people did too, all pushing for floors lower than ours. I wanted to yell at them to cut it out.

When we finally reached the fifth floor, Mr. Spindel was waiting for us. He was wearing the beige janitor uniform he wore at school, the words MR. SPINDEL stenciled on the right chest pocket. He was a wiry man with big hands and usually an easygoing way about him. There was no smile now.

"This way," Mr. Spindel said.

As we followed him, Ema asked, "How is Spoo—I mean, Arthur?"

"No change."

No change. The words hushed the corridor. When we last saw him, Spoon had no feeling in his legs. He was paralyzed below the waist.

No change.

Down the corridor I saw Mrs. Spindel sitting in a chair. I flashed to the first time I had seen her when I dropped Spoon off at his house a few weeks ago. She had greeted her son at the door with such pure joy. Her entire face had lit up as she hugged him. Now it was like someone had extinguished that light. Her cheeks were sunken. Her hair seemed grayer.

Mrs. Spindel gave me a baleful look. The last time I was here, she had told me in no uncertain terms that what happened to her beloved son was my fault. Clearly her opinion had not changed.

"My wife doesn't think this is a good idea," Mr. Spindel explained.

There was no need to comment on that.

We approached a big door.

"I'll wait out here," Mr. Spindel said. "You two go in."

I pushed the heavy door open slowly. Spoon was sitting up in bed. There were tubes and machines and beeping noises.

He looked tiny in that big hospital bed, this little skinny kid with the big glasses lost among all this horror.

When Spoon saw us, his face broke into a huge smile. For a second everything else in the room disappeared. There was just that big smile on the face of that tiny, doofy kid.

"Did you know," Spoon began, "that Babe Ruth wore a cabbage leaf under his baseball cap?"

Ema and I just stood there.

"For real," Spoon went on. "He'd wet it on hot days and it kept him cool. He changed it every two innings."

I couldn't help it. I lost it. I ran over to him and tried so hard not to cry. I'm not a crier by nature. But as I rushed over to Spoon, as I swept him as gently as I could into my arms, I could feel the tears push through my eyelids.

"Mickey?" Spoon said tentatively. "What the . . ."

I squeezed my eyes shut and tried to hold it. I needed to be strong right now. I needed to be strong for Spoon. I was his big, tough friend. I remembered on the very first day we met how he'd said that I was Shrek to his Donkey. I was his protector.

And I had failed him.

It was no use. I started sobbing.

Spoon said, "Mickey?"

"I'm so sorry," I said through the sobs. "I'm so sorry."

"For what?"

I just shook my head and held on to him.

"For what?" Spoon asked again. "You didn't shoot me, did you?"

"No."

"I didn't think so. So what are you sorry about?"

I let him go. I checked his face to see if he was just playing with me, but he looked genuinely baffled.

"It's still my fault," I said.

Spoon frowned. "How on earth do you figure that?"

"Are you serious?"

"As a heart attack," Spoon said. He started laughing. "Man, I always wanted to use that line. Serious as a heart attack, except it really isn't funny, I mean, not in here. Mr. Costo down the hall, he had a heart attack. That's why he's in the hospital. I met his wife. Nice lady. She went to elementary school with Tippi Hedren. You know, the old actress? From *The Birds*? Isn't that something?"

I just looked at him. He smiled again.

"It's okay, Mickey."

I shook my head. "I got you involved in all this."

Spoon pushed the glasses up his nose. "Really?"

I looked at Ema. She shrugged. I turned back to Spoon. "Are you putting me on?"

"No," Spoon said. "And no offense, Mickey, but you're kinda sounding full of yourself."

"What?"

Spoon's eyes met mine. "You're not that powerful, Mickey.

You didn't make me do anything. I made my own choices. I'm my own man." He looked at Ema and winked. "That's why the ladies dig me, am I right?"

Ema rolled her eyes. "Don't make me punch you."

Spoon laughed at that. I just stood there.

"You weren't the only one the Bat Lady chose," Spoon said. "Sure, you're our leader, I guess. But we're a team. We are all a part of Abeona—you, me, Ema. Rachel too. Can we walk away from it? Well, I can't. I mean, I really can't. My legs aren't working right now. But even if they were, I don't think I could. And that has nothing to do with you, Mickey. You're not to blame."

"Wow," I said.

"What?"

"You're kind of making sense."

Spoon arched an eyebrow. "I'm a constant surprise." Another wink for Ema. "Another reason the ladies dig me."

Ema made a fist and showed it to him. Spoon howled with laughter. When he finished, he spread his arms and said, "So?"

"So?" I repeated.

"So why do you think I told my dad I had to see you? We rescue kids. That doesn't stop because I got hurt. So who do we need to rescue now?"

"Just rest," I said. "You need to concentrate on getting better."

Spoon frowned at me and looked toward Ema.

"A guy I met in a chat room," Ema said to him.

"A boyfriend?" Spoon asked.

"Sort of."

Spoon shook his head. "I get shot and you're already on to a new guy?"

"I will hurt you," Ema said.

Spoon pushed the glasses back up his nose again. "Tell me about him," he said.

So she did. Spoon nodded. He never showed doubt. He never judged. He just listened. It made me wonder who indeed was the leader of this group. Ema was just finishing up when a nurse came in and told us it was time to leave.

"I have my laptop," Spoon said. "I'll get us everything I can on this Jared Lowell."

CHAPTER 9

I decided to walk home because I needed to see something.

I cut across Northfield Avenue and tried to clear my head. I made a right on the next corner. I had a destination in mind, even if, in a sense, it no longer existed.

Bat Lady's house.

I know that I shouldn't refer to her as that anymore. The Bat Lady was the name the town kids had given to the creepy, crazy old lady who lives in the creepy, crazy old house, the one that children whispered about and made up stories about and even genuinely feared.

The Bat Lady was not crazy. Or maybe she was, but either way, she was not what any of those kids ever imagined. In a way, the reality behind Bat Lady was even scarier.

The decrepit house that had stood for more than a century was barely more than ashes now. It had been burned down last week. I had been in the house at the time. I had barely escaped with my life. I still didn't know why that man had tried to burn me alive. I had only met him once before.

He was the paramedic who told me that my dad was dead.

I stopped in front of the remains of the house. There was yellow tape surrounding it. I wondered whether that meant that this was a crime scene, if the authorities had figured out that this had been a case of arson, not merely fire.

I flashed back to the day it all started, just a few weeks ago. I had been walking to my new high school, minding my own business, strolling right past this very spot when the front door of the scary old house creaked open.

The Bat Lady had called out to me. "Mickey?"

I had never seen her before. I had no idea how she knew my name.

She pointed a bony finger at me and said the words that changed my life: "Your father isn't dead. He's very much alive."

And then she vanished back inside.

I had thought that his casket would hold the answer. Instead it just led to more questions.

I stared at the remains of the house. Signs reading CONDEMNED and PRIVATE PROPERTY—NO TRESPASSING were everywhere.

So now what?

There were secret tunnels under the house. I wondered whether the fire had affected them. I doubted it. I tried to remember the last time—well, the only time—I had been in them. I knew that the entrance was by the garage, deep in the woods. I knew that they led to the house. I knew that there were other paths underground, a whole maze of them maybe.

Tunnels that had been closed off to me.

Was that all gone now? Or would there be clues down there?

I thought about working my way into the garage and searching for the tunnels, but, no, I couldn't do that right now. For one thing, there were the various KEEP OUT–type signs. But more than that, there were neighbors out and about. A man mowed his lawn. A woman walked her dog. Two girls were drawing on a driveway with chalk. I debated circling around back, trying to find another way into those woods behind Bat Lady's property, when I heard a sweet sound that always got my attention.

The tunnels would have to wait until the street was quiet.

Besides, someone was dribbling a basketball.

The sound called out to me. It worked like a mating call or something. I was drawn to it. The sound was soothing, engaging, comforting, inviting. If someone is dribbling a basketball and you want to join him, you are always welcome. It is part of the code. You could shoot around with someone or rebound for them or take winners. You didn't have to know each other. You didn't have to be the same age or the same sex or play at the same level. All that vanished when someone was dribbling a basketball.

As I drew closer, I could tell from the sound that it was someone practicing alone. Two dribbles. Shot. Two dribbles. Shot. By the speed of it, I'd say that the person was practicing low post moves. The sounds were too close together for outside shots. If you play the game, you'll know what I mean.

When I turned the corner, I saw my team co-captain Brandon Foley taking hook shots in the key. I stopped and watched for a few seconds. He took three from the left, then three from the right, then back to the left. He made nearly every one. His face was coated in sweat. He was concentrating, focused, completely lost in the simple bliss of this drill, but there was something more here, something deeper and not so joyful.

"Hey," I called out.

Brandon stopped and turned toward me. Now I could see that it wasn't sweat coating his face.

It was tears.

"What are you doing here?" he asked me.

"I was just walking by when I heard the dribbling," I said. "Look, I'm sorry about what I said after practice. I appreciate you reaching out like that."

He turned toward the basket and started up his drill again. "Forget it."

I let him shoot for another minute. There was no letup, no slowing down.

"What's wrong?" I asked him.

Brandon dribbled outside and took a shot. The ball swished through the basket and started to roll away. Neither one of us went for it.

"It's all falling apart," Brandon said.

"What is?"

"All these years, all the different teams we played on together, all leading up to this season and now . . ." Brandon shrugged. "It's all gone."

I said nothing. I figured that this had something to do with what I had witnessed with Troy in the locker room, but I didn't want to let on that I'd seen.

"Everything was going so well," Brandon said. "We had all worked so hard and prepared and then, today, your very first day on the team and . . ."

He didn't finish the thought. He didn't have to. His glare said it all.

"Wait, are you blaming me?"

Brandon turned back toward the basket and started shooting again.

"So what happened?" I asked him.

"Troy and Buck," he said.

My two sworn enemies.

"What about them?"

"They're both off the team."

"What?"

Brandon nodded. "That's right. Troy was our leading scorer. Buck was our best defender. Both gone."

"Why?" I asked.

"What do you care?" He took another hook shot. "Heck, you're probably happy. It clears two spots for you."

I moved toward the basket. I grabbed the ball and held on to it. "I wanted to earn a spot," I said. "I don't want to get it because other guys drop out."

Brandon looked off for a second. He let loose a deep breath and wiped his face with his forearm. "I'm sorry," he said, his voice softening. "I'm snapping at you, but I know this isn't your fault."

"So what happened?"

"Buck moved."

"What? Now?"

Brandon nodded. "See, his parents got divorced when we were all in eighth grade. He's lived with his father and brother, but now his parents decided he should be with his mom."

"Just like that?" I asked. "During his senior year of high school?"

"I guess. I don't know. I never heard a hint of it until today."

Part of me was pleased, of course. I hated Buck, and Buck hated me. But this somehow didn't feel right. "So that's why Buck wasn't at practice," I said.

"Yeah."

"And Troy?"

Brandon put up his right hand, inviting me to throw him the pass. I did. He grabbed the ball in his outstretched hand, took one dribble, and dunked it hard through the hoop.

"He's been suspended for the season," Brandon said.

"For what?"

"Steroids."

My mouth dropped open in surprise. "He failed a drug test?"

"Yes."

"Wow," I said, but now I understood what I had witnessed in the locker room. Coach Grady must have just given him the news.

"Troy swears he's never taken anything like that," Brandon said. "He says he's being set up."

I remembered hearing him claim that in the locker room. "How could that be?"

"I don't know."

"And who would do that?" I asked. "I mean, the testing all seems pretty much on the up-and-up."

"I know," Brandon said.

Brandon threw me the ball. I took a shot. "Do you believe Troy?" I asked him.

Brandon grabbed the rebound, threw me the ball. I took another shot, waiting for his answer. He seemed to be chewing over the question.

"Troy is a lot of things," he said. "I know he can be, well, rough around the edges. I even know that he can be a bully. But a liar? A drug cheat?"

We both stopped and looked at each other.

"Yeah," Brandon said, "I know it's crazy, but I believe Troy."

CHAPTER 10

I wanted to go back to the Bat Lady's house that night, but here was the problem: I had too much homework. I'd been blowing it off for days now, and if I didn't start working on the essay for history and study for the math quiz, I'd be in huge trouble. I turned off my mobile phone, sat at the kitchen table, and got to work.

First thing Tuesday morning, I had history with my favorite teacher, Mrs. Friedman. Rachel's desk was empty. I didn't know what to think, but it really wasn't a huge surprise. There had been a shooting at her house. Her mother ended up dead, and Rachel ended up hospitalized with a bullet wound. The wound ended up being minor. Physically she was okay. Mentally, well, that was another story.

I had been the one to tell Rachel the truth. I had been warned by her father not to, but Uncle Myron had given me other advice, warning me that if you lie, it never leaves the room. It haunts the relationship forever. That made sense to me, so I ended up listening to Myron.

Rachel and I hadn't communicated since, and yet if I had to do it all again . . . I don't know.

The vibe in the school cafeteria was decidedly somber today. Ema and I sat at our usual table in what is often dubbed "Loserville." Our table could sit twelve, but today there were just the two of us. Usually we were three, and staring at the spot where Spoon normally sat made my chest hurt.

"I'm worried about him too," Ema said. "But he wouldn't want us moping around about it."

I nodded. I had met Spoon in this very cafeteria. He had walked up to me and offered me his spoon for reasons I still didn't get. In my mind I had started thinking of him as "that spoon kid," which had been shortened to Spoon. Spoon loved the nickname and insisted that we use it always and forever. If someone called him Arthur now, he ignored them.

The tables with the kids we deem more popular for whatever dumb reasons were usually an active beehive of varsity jackets, blond highlights, loud voices, big laughs, and enthusiastic high fives. But not today. Troy was still there, at the head of the table as usual, but he was quiet. The rest of the table followed his mood. In fact, it seemed as though the whole cafeteria were in silent mourning over the recent fate of their fallen leader.

"It's so quiet in here," Ema said.

She and I were always on the same wavelength.

"Too quiet," I said, arching a joking eyebrow.

I wasn't suicidal enough to smile or laugh out loud, but I didn't want to be a hypocrite. I hated Troy with pretty good reason, and that wasn't about to change over this. Yes, I understood how painful it must be to lose a season of basketball, especially now, in your last year of playing with your buddies. But then again, some of us had never had a steady group of buddies to play with. Some of us hadn't been handed those opportunities, just to toss them away.

I didn't feel sorry for him.

Troy had cheated by taking PEDs—performance-enhancing drugs. I didn't buy Brandon's defense. That was what every athlete said when they were caught—it was a mistake, it was a fix, it wasn't me. I would probably admire Troy more if he just admitted it. Whatever. It wasn't my business.

Troy's table was usually full, but the seat next to his, the one where Buck always sat, was empty. I could usually count on Buck to be staring me down, mouthing that I was a "dead man," emphasizing the point by making a slashing motion across his neck with his finger. Buck would then make fun of Ema in some cruel way, call her "fugly" or moo at her, a classic insecure bully idiot. I wouldn't miss him either.

But I did find it odd.

Troy and Buck had been best friends since elementary school. Suddenly, within a few days of one another, Troy had been caught up in a drug scandal and Buck had moved away.

I lowered my head to start eating when I realized that the room had suddenly gone even quieter if possible, as though everyone had decided to hold their breath at the same time.

Then I heard Ema said, "Whoa."

I lifted my head and felt the familiar jolt.

Rachel Caldwell had entered the cafeteria.

The silence was for a few reasons. One, this was her first return to school since the shooting that had left her mother dead and Rachel wounded. That had been our last . . . I don't know what the word is . . . case, I guess, for the Abeona Shelter. We had solved it, but the answer remained a carefully guarded secret.

I hadn't even told Ema.

I felt bad about that. Ema and Spoon had risked their lives and done everything anyone could have asked. They were my best friends and I hated the idea of keeping secrets from them, especially Ema, but in this case, the secret wasn't mine to tell. It was Rachel's. If I tell Ema, I betray Rachel. But then again, by not telling Ema . . .

In the end, I hoped and believed that Ema would understand. But I could be wrong about that.

I had not seen Rachel since the day I flew to California, when I showed up at her door and blew her world apart.

Reason Two for the cafeteria silence: Rachel was a popular girl. More to the point, she was captain of the cheerleading team, the hottest girl in school, the girl everyone talked about—you get the drift. People paid attention to a girl like that.

Reason Three: Rachel and Troy had been—I start gagging when I even think of it—an item. Rachel made it clear to me that she'd been young and dumb and that it was way, *way* over, though maybe she should make it a little clearer to Troy.

Still, I couldn't help but notice that she wasn't coming over to say hi to Ema or me. She was heading for Troy's table. She took Buck's seat—the one next to him—and forced up a sad smile for Troy.

My face felt hot.

"Stop it," Ema whispered to me.

"What?"

She just frowned at me and shook her head. "Troy was just kicked off the basketball team. She has to show some kind of support for him, don't you think?"

I didn't. But that wasn't the point. Rachel hadn't so much as glanced in our direction. Ema wouldn't understand why. But I did. Uncle Myron had warned me that there would be a price for telling the truth, but how had he put it?

The ugliest truth is still better than the prettiest of lies.

She was avoiding me. I don't know what advice someone would give me about that. *Give her time,* probably. I had done that already. Not a lot of time. But enough. Besides, I had learned that "giving time" often meant "time to fester."

I needed to confront Rachel. The sooner, the better.

CHAPTER 11

I made it my business to walk past Rachel's locker between classes, hoping to catch her there. Finally, with only one period left in the day, I found her, but she was far from alone. Rachel's locker was surrounded by cheerleaders and jocks and a potpourri of popular kids, all welcoming her back and showing concern.

I didn't know them. They didn't know me.

I was the new kid and so there was some natural curiosity about me. My height also drew attention, I think, and maybe I was starting to get a rep for my basketball. I had, of course, lost a lot of popularity cred by choosing to hang out with Ema and Spoon. So now maybe I was less a curiosity and more an oddity.

Rachel saw me approach and gave a slow shake of her

head. I got the meaning. *Stay away.* I should have respected that, nodded in return and moved on my way.

I didn't. I stood there and mouthed the word, *When?*

Her reply was a slammed locker. Rachel shot me one last dagger, turned, and strolled away.

Terrific.

My final period today was health with Mr. Nacht, a class that couldn't be more snooze worthy if it included Benadryl. When classes ended, I hurried back to Rachel's locker. No sign of her. I went to my own. I had basketball practice in half an hour, but it would be good to get there early and work on my shooting. I reached into my locker and grabbed my phone. There was a message from Spoon: **Got some information on Jared. Stop by tonight.**

There was another buzz. Again it was Spoon, the boy who lived for irrelevant factoids: **Porcupines float in water.**

Good to know, in case I was ever tempted to rescue a water-drenched porcupine.

I was first changed and out on the gym floor. I shot around, enjoying the solo echo of one man dribbling and shooting. The other guys started to sputter out of the locker room. None chose to shoot with me. I was hardly surprised. Normally there was laughter, horsing around, banter, whatever. Not today. The gym was silent as a tomb—or the cafeteria today. The only sounds came from the bouncing balls.

At four o'clock, Coach Grady blew the whistle and shouted

for everyone to take a seat. Brandon and some guy I hadn't met yet pulled out the rickety accordion-like stands. We all climbed up a step or two and found a place to sit.

Coach Grady looked as though he'd aged ten years since last practice. He paced for a few moments. We all sat and watched him. Behind him, Coach Stashower held a clipboard and waited.

"We have our work cut out for us," Coach Grady said. "As most of you know by now, Troy has been suspended from the team. He has the right to appeal, which he has taken, but in the meantime he will not be allowed to practice or play with the team. Troy had been our co-captain. During his absence, which will last the entire season if it's not overturned on appeal—and frankly I don't know anyone who has ever won an appeal—Brandon will serve as our solo captain."

All eyes turned to Brandon. Brandon kept his head up, his face set.

"On top of that, Buck's family has decided that he would be better off living with his mother, so he won't be with us for the season. That means two seniors, both starters and leaders on last year's team, won't be playing with us this season. I don't think I have to tell you what a big blow this is for our program."

Coach Grady adjusted the cap on his head and let loose a long sigh. "But victory often comes out of adversity. We can give up, or we can rise to the challenge. For many of you, there is an opportunity here to step up. For us as a team, we can either let these setbacks tear us to shreds—or make us more cohesive. We can either come together or come apart."

He put his foot up on the lowest bench, leaned onto his knee, and took a few seconds to scan our faces. "I believe in all of you. I believe in this team. And I believe we can still achieve great things this season."

Absolute silence.

"Okay, boys, take three laps and start the three-man weave. Let's go."

He clapped his hands, and we were off.

The practice did not go well. If I'd hoped that Troy being vanquished would help me, I was very sadly mistaken. If anything, the rest of the guys seemed extra angry with me, as if it were my fault. They froze me out. They threw passes at my feet. Someone hit me with a dirty elbow. I fought through it and played hard, but part of me wanted to just quit.

When practice ended, I was a sweaty mess, but I didn't want to hang around these guys one second longer than necessary. I was about to head out when Brandon ran up behind me.

"Mickey?"

I turned toward him.

"We need to talk," he said.

"Uh, okay. Now?"

He came a little closer. "Let's wait for the other guys to leave. I don't want them to see us. Shower, get dressed, take your time."

So I did. Again everyone avoided me, except to give me

death stares. Half an hour later, Brandon and I were the only ones left in the locker room.

"So talk," I said to him.

Brandon looked left, then right. "Not here," he whispered. "Follow me."

"Where?"

"Just follow me."

He held open the door, inviting me out into the still corridor. I didn't like it. The players and coaches were gone now. So were all the teachers. Our footsteps echoed down hallway.

"You get what's going on, right?" Brandon said.

"About?"

"About why the guys on the team are mad at you."

"No."

"Think about it."

I did. I still didn't get it.

"You join the team," Brandon said, "and suddenly Troy comes up with a positive drug test."

"So?" Then: "Wait, are you saying people think I had something to do with it?"

Brandon nodded. "We've all known Troy for years. He's a lot of things. But he's not a drug cheat."

"So, what, they think I spiked his urine or something?"

Brandon stopped and looked at me. "Did you?"

"Are you out of your mind?"

"Did you?"

"Of course not. Seriously, even if I wanted to, how would I?"

Brandon shrugged. "You have access to the school."

"What are you talking about?"

"People know you're friends with the janitor's weird kid."

He meant Spoon. I was about to defend Spoon, to snap back that Spoon wasn't weird, but then I remembered something: Spoon was weird. Wonderfully so. But he was weird.

"He's got keys, right? He could sneak you into places."

"To alter drug tests?" I said. "That's insane."

"Is it? Heck, you guys were in here with drug dealers last week. The janitor's kid got shot, right?"

"Right, but—"

"There's been a lot of crazy stuff happening in this town since you moved in," Brandon said, "and somehow, Mickey, you seem to always be in the middle of it."

We were in a dark corridor now. I didn't like it. I didn't like any of this.

"Where are we going, Brandon?"

"Almost there."

When we reached the end of the corridor, I heard a familiar voice say, "Hello, Mickey. Thanks for coming."

I turned.

It was Troy.

CHAPTER 12

I took two steps back and debated how to play this.

I could make a run for it. I could stand and fight. I wasn't afraid. I was pretty good with my fists, but then again it was two against one, at the very least. There might be more of them somewhere nearby. I could also go after one, make a quick strike, and sprint down the corridor.

But neither Troy nor Brandon moved toward me. They just stood there, both looking at each other nervously, then back at me.

"What's going on?" I asked.

"We need to talk," Brandon said. "That's all. Just talk."

"Are you going to start up again with that nonsense about me setting up Troy?"

It was Troy who replied. "No. I didn't believe it for a second."

I looked at him. For the first time since we'd met, Troy Taylor wasn't looking at me with naked hostility. He wasn't telling me I was a dead man. He wasn't mooing at Ema. He looked like a real, live human being.

"I need your help, Mickey."

"Me?"

Brandon stepped forward. "All that stuff I said before. About how you could break into the school. About all that stuff you've been involved with."

"What about it?"

Troy and Brandon exchanged another look. "You're good at stuff like that."

"What are you talking about?"

"Come on, Mickey," Troy said. "My dad is the chief of police here, remember?"

Boy, did I know. Chief Taylor probably hated me more than his son did.

"He told me how you were doing your own investigation when that girl Ashley disappeared. He told me that you drove a car and broke into a nightclub down in Newark. I know you helped Rachel figure out who shot her and her mom. You were actually here, in this school, when those bad guys shot up the place, and you came out on the winning end."

Winning end, I thought. Spoon lay partially paralyzed in the hospital and Rachel was devastated. Some winning end.

"I still don't see your point," I said.

Troy looked at Brandon. Brandon nodded at him to continue.

"You're like some kind of kid detective," Troy said. "I don't know. But I need your help."

"Help with what?"

"I need you to help me prove that I didn't take steroids."

"Me?" I glanced at Brandon and then back at Troy. "You're kidding, right?"

Brandon said, "Just hear him out."

"I didn't do it, Mickey. I swear."

I still couldn't believe what I was hearing. "First off, Troy, I don't believe you. But even if I did, you've been nothing but a bully to me since I arrived. You pick on my friends. You tried to hurt me at practice."

"I know that. And I'm sorry."

"That's not good enough."

"Mickey?"

"What?"

Troy spread his arms. "We're teammates, right?"

I said nothing.

"This is what teammates do. We help each other. Like family. And, yeah, Mickey, maybe you'll be the star this year. Maybe you'll even score more points than me. I don't know. But you know the team will have a better chance of winning the state championship if I'm on it."

I shuffled my feet. "This isn't my business," I said.

"Mickey, look at me for a second. Okay? Just look at me."

I did.

"I'm sorry," Troy said again. "I was getting on your case because you're new to the school and you're only a sopho- more and, okay, maybe I was jealous. I mean, you just came to this school and you're this hotshot basketball star and, well, already my girl is spending more time with you than me."

I was about to comment on that, but Brandon just shook his head at me, signaling for me to let it go.

"So here I am," Troy said, "asking for your help."

I wasn't sure how to respond. I took a step back. "As you pointed out, your father is the chief of police," I said. "Let him help you."

"He can't do this."

"Sure he can."

"I need someone with your skills. I need someone who gets it, who's part of the team."

I almost bought into it right then—the idea of team. But then I remembered it all. Troy's threats, the way he bullied Spoon and grabbed Ema's laptop, how he had set me up and almost got me thrown off the team, the way he yelled "moooo" and cackled whenever Ema walked by him in the cafeteria.

"I'm sorry," Troy repeated. He stuck out his hand. "Can't we start again?"

"I have to go," I said.

Brandon said, "Mickey . . ."

"This isn't my battle, Brandon. You kept saying how I get in the middle of these things. This time I'm staying out of it."

I turned and started down the corridor.

CHAPTER 13

Brandon caught up to me when I reached the door. "Cold," he said.

"It's like sixty degrees out," I said.

"Ha, ha. I meant the way you just dissed Troy."

"You're joking, right? You were there when he whipped the ball at my face. How long ago was that? Oh, that's right. Last practice."

"He was jealous. He explained that to you. Don't you get that at all? You've spent your life traveling around. You don't know what it's like when you're in a town like this. Things are just expected of you. And for Troy, well, he's been the best basketball player in town. His dad's the chief of police. He had this great girlfriend—and yeah, yeah, I know, you didn't take her away—but suddenly someone comes in and threatens everything he's worked for. Don't you have any compassion at all?"

I thought about that. "He was mean to my friends."

"Because they're an extension of you."

Again with the justifying. "And seriously, Brandon, what can I do anyway? His dad should help him."

"Troy's dad can't help."

"Why not?"

"Because," Brandon said, "his dad doesn't believe him."

That surprised me. "What?"

"That's right. Even his own father has abandoned him on this. He thinks his son cheated. Chief Taylor wants to see if Troy can get back on the team in other ways, you know, come clean, say it's a first offense. But Troy doesn't want that. He wants his name cleared. He wants the truth to come out."

I didn't know what to say.

"There's something else you should consider too," Brandon said.

"What?"

"Your teammates, like it or not, think you had something to do with Troy's suspension."

"But even Troy said he knew I had nothing to do with it."

"And maybe he'll tell the other guys that. Or maybe he won't. Maybe he'll wonder why you rejected his peace offering and slapped his hand away. Maybe he'll start to think the rest of the guys are right about you."

I said nothing.

"You see what I'm saying?"

"I think so. It sounds like blackmail. Help Troy or look like the guy who set him up."

"That's putting it too strongly," Brandon said. "More like, help Troy and look like the kind of teammate other guys want to play with. Look like the kind of teammate other guys respect and look up to and want to be around. Look like the kind of teammate who stands up for his captain, even when it's hard."

"Wow," I said.

"What?"

"No wonder you're always elected class president."

Brandon smiled and put his hand on my shoulder. "Help him, Mickey. Help yourself. Help your team."

And because I'm a complete idiot, I told him that I would.

CHAPTER 14

Ema did not take it well.

"Are you out of your mind?" Ema asked.

We were entering the lobby of the hospital, heading up to Spoon's room.

"If you'd just listen a second—"

"Oh, I heard you. You want to help Troy Taylor! Troy Freakin' Taylor!" She spread her arms. "What, are there no serial killers who need our help?"

"Forget it. I'll do it on my own, okay?"

"No, not okay. We work together. That's part of this. And we have more pressing problems, thank you very much."

"You mean your"—I tried to say it without sounding sarcastic—"boyfriend?"

"Are you being sarcastic?"

Like I said, I tried.

"It'd be a waste of time anyway," Ema said.

"Why?"

"Because you know Troy's guilty."

"A lot of people don't think so."

"Like who? Brandon? Look, Brandon is a nice guy, but he's always been under Troy's spell."

"I may need to do it," I said.

"Need?"

"To help me."

"Help you how?"

"To help get my teammates to see me in a new light."

She blinked. "Are you serious?"

"They hate me, Ema. All of them."

"And you think helping Troy will do what exactly? Make all the jocks think you're cool?"

"No," I said.

"Because if you want to be cool, your best bet is to jettison the uncool people around you."

"Will you stop it?"

We got into the elevator.

"I still don't understand," Ema said. "What do you want out of this?"

I opened my mouth, closed it, tried again. There was no point. She wouldn't understand. "Do you get what basketball means to me?"

Ema met my gaze and moved closer. I felt something warm pass over me. "Yes, of course."

"You can't be an outsider on a team," I said. "You can't be the loner sitting at a table in the corner."

"You mean like I do?"

"No, I mean like *we* do. Basketball is a team sport. That's the beauty of it. I want to be a part of that. It's why I wanted my parents to settle in one place. So I could play on a real team. So I could know what that's like—being part of a team and all that goes along with it."

I stopped because the emotion came suddenly. Suppose I hadn't wanted that. Suppose I had just kept my mouth shut. Would my dad be alive (or with me)? Would my mom have stayed off drugs?

Had my desire to be part of a real team destroyed everything?

"I know that's what you want, Mickey," Ema said in the softest voice. "I get that. But helping Troy Taylor—"

"Will show everyone that I'm willing to do *anything* to be a good teammate."

Ema shook her head, but she didn't argue.

We reached the door to Spoon's hospital room. No one was around, so I knocked lightly and pushed it open. I heard Spoon's voice:

"Did you know that ants stretch when they wake up in the morning?"

I smiled. Ah, Spoon.

"Oh, and I mean ant like the insect. Not aunts like my aunt Tessie. She never stretches."

I wondered what nurse or doctor he was regaling with his random facts, but when I saw who it was, I pulled up short.

It was Rachel.

Spoon smiled at us from the bed. "Great," he said. "We're all here."

Rachel greeted Ema with a brief hug but only nodded at me and turned away. Ema looked at me, puzzled. Rachel was usually much friendlier with me, but of course, Ema didn't know about our last conversation, when I told her the truth about her mother's death.

"Four of us," Spoon said. "Do you know that the number four is considered unlucky in many East Asian cultures? That's because the word for four sounds like the word for death."

He pushed his glasses up his nose.

"Spooky, right?"

Ema sighed and said, "Did you find anything about Jared Lowell?"

Before he could answer, the door behind us opened. A nurse in pink hospital scrubs stepped into the room. She did not look pleased to see us. "What is this?"

Spoon spread his arms. "My posse."

"Your what?"

"My posse. These are my peeps, my crew, my homies—"

"Are they immediate family?"

"More than immediate family," Spoon said. "They're my posse, my peeps, my crew, my—"

The nurse was having none of it. "You're only allowed one non-family visitor at a time, Arthur. You know that."

Spoon frowned. "But I had two here yesterday."

"Then someone was breaking the rules. I need two of you to leave this room immediately."

We all looked at one another, not sure what to do. Spoon took care of it.

"I will talk to all three of you separately, but—and I hope you lovely ladies don't consider this in any way to be sexist—Mickey and I first need to have a man-to-man talk."

He winked at me. I tried not to frown. Ema did not look pleased. I got that. She was the one most interested in finding Jared Lowell.

"I can wait," I said. "You and Ema can go first."

Spoon shook his head. "Man to man. It's important."

He looked at me hard, trying to send a message. I noticed now that the call button was near his right hand. I wondered whether he had pressed it—whether that was the reason why the nurse had suddenly appeared.

The nurse clapped her hands. "Okay, ladies, you heard the man. Let's leave them alone for their *bro* talk." She gestured toward the door, escorting Ema and Rachel out into the corridor.

Spoon and I were alone.

"Did you call for the nurse?" I asked.

"Yep."

"Why?"

"I wanted to show you what I found before we tell Ema."

"Why? He's a fake, right? Jared Lowell."

"No. Her boyfriend, Jared, is very much real. Maybe too real."

"What do you mean?"

Spoon pressed the button next to his bed so that he could sit more upright. "Jared Lowell's residence is in Massachusetts, a small place called Adiona Island."

"Lie Number One," I said.

"What?"

"He told Ema that he lives in Connecticut."

"Well, he does. Sorta. That's why I used the word *residence*. Jared Lowell actually lives at the Farnsworth School, a fancy-shmancy prep school in Connecticut. All boys. They have to wear a jacket and tie every day. Could you imagine? That would put a crimp in my fashion statements, I think. I'm normally known in school as a pretty natty dresser, right?"

"Natty?"

"Sharp. I'm a sharp dresser, don't you think?"

To keep Spoon on track, I said, "I do."

"Anyway, Jared Lowell is seventeen years old and a senior. He does indeed have a Facebook page, but he almost never used it—not until recently anyway. After he, uh, disappeared or whatever, he took down almost all the photographs on his page. You know this already, right?"

"I guess," I said.

"So have you seen any pictures of him?" Spoon asked.

"Just the profile picture."

"So you probably don't know that he's tall."

I didn't see the relevance. "Okay."

Spoon looked me in the eye. "He's six-four."

My height. "Okay," I said again.

"Or that he plays basketball. In fact, he's the leading scorer for his high school team, averaging nineteen points per game."

I nodded and said, "Okay."

"Or that his father's dead, so he only has his mother."

I stopped saying okay.

"Did you notice that Jared kinda looks like you?"

"He doesn't look like me," I said.

"He's more pretty-boy. You're more what the ladies would call rugged. But, yeah, Mickey, there are similarities. Lots of them."

"So what's your point, Spoon?"

"No point. I just find it interesting that Ema fell for a guy who could be, well, you."

I said nothing.

"Mickey?"

"What do you want me to say here, Spoon? We're both tall and play basketball. I don't attend a fancy-shmancy private school. I'm only a sophomore, not a senior. I don't live with my mother—she's in rehab, remember?"

Spoon nodded. "That's all true."

"And this is still feeling like a catfish to me. You were able to independently confirm that Jared Lowell is real?"

"Yes. There are articles on his ball playing, complete with photographs and statistics. He's real."

"I'm still thinking this is a catfish," I said. "All the stuff you said, okay, there are similarities. So someone—maybe Troy or Buck or some other toad—found this guy online and made up a fake Facebook page—"

"No," Spoon said.

"How's that?"

"The Facebook page has existed for four years. It's a little hard to explain, but the original setup ISP originated on Adiona Island—where he lives. He also used it. Not a lot. He isn't a big Facebook guy. But it was in use and the posts are obviously not fake."

"So Jared Lowell is real?"

"Yes."

"And his Facebook page is his?"

"Yes."

I pointed my palms to the sky. "So where is he now?"

"Normally I would say there is no big mystery."

"Meaning?"

"Meaning there are no articles or indications that he's missing. I assume he's at school. If he was hurt or vanished, I think there would be something online, don't you?"

"I do," I said.

"All we know for certain is that he's not currently using his

Facebook page and has stopped communicating with Ema. Normally I would say that this doesn't concern us. For whatever reason, he decided that Ema wasn't for him and, well, was less than a gentleman about informing her."

"Normally."

"Right."

"So why isn't this 'normally'?"

"Because nothing about us is normal, Mickey," Spoon said. "You know that."

I did.

"And while many photographs were taken down from his Facebook page, only one has been added since he stopped talking to Ema."

I nodded. "The Abeona butterfly."

"Right."

I sighed. "So we need to see this through."

"Right again. Unless."

"Unless what?"

"We have our enemies, don't we, Mickey?"

I thought about the sandy-haired paramedic with the green eyes. He had taken my father away from the car accident. He had set Bat Lady's house—Abeona's headquarters—on fire while I was inside.

"We do," I said.

"He could be another. Jared Lowell. This could be a setup."

Spoon could be right. But it gave me another idea. "Do you remember this?"

I handed him the old black-and-white photograph. The man dressed in the Nazi uniform was, I'd been told at first, the Butcher of Lodz, a monstrous war criminal who had killed hundreds, maybe thousands, during World War II. But it wasn't. At least not entirely.

The face belonged to the paramedic with the sandy hair and green eyes.

For a long time, I had been bewildered by this—how could a Nazi from World War II have been the paramedic who wheeled away my dad? But sometimes the simplest answer is so close to us, we can't see.

The paramedic's face had been Photoshopped onto the Butcher of Lodz's body by the Bat Lady.

I still had no idea who he was.

"Sure," Spoon said. "What about it?"

I put my finger right on the picture's face. "You know he's not really the Butcher of Lodz, right?"

"Right."

"Is there any way you can figure out who he really is?"

Spoon studied the picture. He started to nod slowly. "I think maybe I can. Let me work on it, okay?"

"Okay."

Spoon put the photograph in the drawer next to his bed. "You better let Ema in now. What do you think I should tell her?"

"The truth," I said.

I looked down at him, in that bed, paralyzed below the

waist. I was blocking on that. It was the only way to stay upright. But suddenly I felt the tears building again. Spoon looked up at me and then turned away.

"Arthur?" I said.

"Don't call me that," he said.

"Spoon?"

"What?"

I swallowed. "How are you? Really."

He gave me the big smile. "Terrific!"

I just looked at him and waited. The smile faded away.

"To tell the truth," Spoon said, "I'm a little scared."

"Yeah," I said. "I get that."

Silence.

"Mickey?"

"Yeah?"

"After I talk to the girls, do you think you can hang in my room for a while?"

I managed not to cry. "For as long as you'd like."

CHAPTER 15

Ema went in next, leaving Rachel and me alone for the first time since I knocked on the door and told her the truth about her mother's death. For a few minutes we avoided each other's gaze. I stood there feeling ridiculously awkward, shuffling my feet, casually fake whistling. I had no idea why I was fake whistling, but that's what I was doing. I bounced on my toes. My hands felt really big and like I had no place to put them. I jammed them in my pockets.

Rachel was beautiful. It was as simple as that. Physically she was the complete package. Everyone thought so. At our school, she was "that" girl, but I've often found that the "high school hot," while obviously attractive, can often have looks that are somewhat blank or standard or like some kind of formula—that when you are universally considered hot, that hotness can also be bland.

That wasn't the case here. Rachel's beauty was, well, interesting.

I moved toward her hesitantly, half expecting her to shake her head for me to go away again. She smelled great, like honeysuckle and lilacs.

"Hey," I said, because I'm smooth like that.

"Hey."

"Are you okay?" I asked.

"Fine."

Silence.

"I'm sorry," I said.

"It's not your fault."

"Your father thought it'd be better if you didn't know the truth. He didn't want me to tell you what happened to your mom."

Rachel tilted her head. "So why did you?"

I hadn't expected her to ask that. I guess that I expected to get credit for being honest, but her eyes were pinning me down, wanting an answer.

"It was something my uncle said."

"Your uncle Myron?"

"Yes."

"What?"

"It was about lies. Even when they're for someone's good."

"Go on."

"I don't remember his exact words, but he said that it might be a good lie, it might be a bad lie, but either way, the lie would always be in the room with us."

Rachel nodded. I wanted to ask more. I wanted to know how her father had reacted, but it wasn't my place to ask. We stood in silence for a few more seconds. I broke it:

"I was surprised to see you here. Did Spoon call you?"

"No," she said.

"So how did you know to come?"

"This was in my locker."

Rachel handed me an essay she had written for Mrs. Friedman's history class. She had gotten an A with a comment in Mrs. Friedman's script saying, "Great job!" But that wasn't the important thing. The important thing was the image someone had stamped onto the top right-hand corner of the first page.

The Abeona butterfly.

"Did you do this?" she asked.

I sighed. "You know better."

"So who was it?"

"I don't know. And yet we all know."

Rachel shook her head. "You sound like a fortune cookie." She looked toward Spoon's door. "So there's another kid who's missing."

"Maybe. What did Spoon tell you before we got here?"

"That Thomas Jefferson had a pet mockingbird and when he was alone in his study, he'd close the door and let the bird fly around."

I smiled.

"So who's missing?"

"A guy Ema met online. His name is Jared Lowell."

I filled her in on what I knew. When I finished, I said, "Can I ask you a personal question?"

"Sure."

"Are you and Troy . . . ?"

"No. You of all people should understand."

"Understand what?"

"He loves basketball like *you* love basketball."

And it had been taken away from him in his final year. Troy was maybe good enough to play college, get a scholarship even, and now it was all gone.

"Do you think he did it?" I asked.

"Took steroids?"

"Yeah," I said. "He says he was set up."

"Is that possible?" Rachel asked.

"I don't know. You know him"—ugh—"well. I want your opinion."

"Why do you care what I think?" she asked.

"Because he asked me to investigate it."

Rachel's eyes widened. "What?"

"Troy wants me to prove that the test was wrong or fixed or whatever."

"You?"

"My reaction exactly."

She shook her head. "Wow."

"So?"

"I don't know," she said. "I never knew him to cheat. He was overly competitive, for sure. He has a lot of pressure on him and, yeah, maybe he's been acting out more. But a cheater? I don't think so."

Ema came out and Rachel went in. A few minutes later, Rachel exited the room. We were all going to leave together, but I told them that I needed to stay behind with Spoon for a while. They understood and started home.

I entered Spoon's room nervously, but he immediately put me at ease. We laughed a lot. Life was funny, I thought. The most poignant moments always ended up being the most mixed. I had a great time with Spoon even while my heart broke. Laughter can be more intense when it's blended with tears.

It was getting late, but I didn't want to leave him. I texted Uncle Myron and explained what was going on. He understood: **I'll pick you up when you're done. Don't worry about the hour.**

I told him not to wait up—that I'd walk—and then I turned off the phone before he could argue. Time passed. Spoon put a sitcom on the television. At some point, I realized that he had stopped speaking, which was something that never happened. I turned toward him.

Spoon had fallen asleep.

I watched him. Lots of emotions passed through me. I didn't stop or analyze them. I just let them flow through. I felt my eyes grow heavy. I decided that I would close them for a minute, no more, and then I would make sure Spoon was okay and head home. That was my plan anyway. Rest the eyes for a second.

I don't know how much time passed. It may have been an hour. It may have been more. I was dreaming about the car accident that killed my father, the sound of brakes screeching, the crunch of impact, the way my body flew. I saw my father lying on the ground, bleeding, his eyes closed, and that paramedic, that damn paramedic with the sandy-blond hair and green eyes, meeting my eye . . .

A hand touched my shoulder.

"Mickey?"

My blood went cold. I jerked awake. I was back in Spoon's hospital room. It was dark. He was asleep. The hand was still on my shoulder. I turned in my chair and looked up at the silhouette of the nurse. Except of course it wasn't a nurse. I knew that the moment I heard her voice.

It was the Bat Lady.

CHAPTER 16

I had a million questions to ask her.

Bat Lady kept her hand on my shoulder. The hand was bony with liver spots and thick veins. I knew that she had to be well into her eighties by now. She looked it. And I knew that I should stop thinking of her as Bat Lady. Her real name was Elizabeth "Lizzy" Sobek. Her whole family died during the Holocaust, but young Lizzy had saved a group of children from certain death in a concentration camp in Poland. After that, the famous teen became a resistance fighter against the Nazi occupation.

No one heard from her again.

Most history books believe that she'd been killed during World War II.

Most history books are wrong.

"Are you okay?" I asked her.

The last time I was in her house, the sandy-haired man with the green eyes burned it to the ground. I had not seen her since.

"I'm fine," she said.

She loomed over me, looking larger and stronger than she had in the past. Maybe that was because she had traded in her tattered, long white nightgown for hospital scrubs. The gray hair that normally flowed down past her shoulders was tied into a bun.

She made her way toward the front of Spoon's bed and checked his chart. Her face looked grim.

"Can't you do something?" I asked. "He can't walk."

"I'm not a doctor, Mickey."

"But can't you . . . ?"

"No," she said. She moved toward Spoon's head. She reached down and smoothed back his hair. "I'm sorry."

"That's not good enough."

"It never is."

"It's our fault," I said.

"Perhaps." She turned toward me. "We save many, but there is always a cost."

I gestured toward the bed. "He shouldn't be the one to pay for it."

She almost smiled. "Do you want to lecture me about how life isn't fair, Mickey?"

"No, ma'am." I shifted in the chair. "Where have you been?"

"That's not important." She looked down at Spoon. "He's meant for great things, you know."

"So he's going to be okay?"

"I didn't say that." She turned toward me. "My house is gone."

"The paramedic. He burned it down."

"I know."

"He tried to kill me."

She didn't respond to that.

"I still don't understand." I opened up the drawer next to Spoon's bed and pulled out the old black-and-white picture. "Why did you give me this?"

She didn't respond to that either.

"You told me that it's the Butcher of Lodz from World War Two," I said, trying to control my anger. "But that's not who it is at all. I mean, the body is, I guess. But the face . . . that's the paramedic who told me that my dad was dead. Why did you give this to me?"

"The Butcher of Lodz killed my family," she said.

"I know."

"This man," she said. "He is your Butcher."

I shook my head. "So he's, what, my enemy?"

She said nothing.

"And I still don't get why you put his face on this body."

"It was," she said, "a test."

"How so?"

"I wanted to see your reaction. I needed to see if you were on our side. Or his."

"Wait, you're not making any sense. Who is he?"

"The last time you were in my house, you went upstairs, yes?"

I nodded.

"You saw the Hall of the Rescued."

"Is that what you call it?"

"You saw it?"

I had seen it. When I went up the stairs of the old house, the hallway had been blanketed with pictures of children and teenagers. Hundreds, thousands, maybe tens of thousands. They'd been everywhere, crawling up both walls, clinging to the ceiling. There were layers upon layers of them. Some were black and white. Some were color. There were so many of them, you couldn't find the walls or the ceiling.

Only photographs of the children.

Missing children. Check that: rescued children.

"The pictures were burned in the fire," I said.

"I know."

"I still don't get it," I said. "What do the pictures have to do with the guy?"

"If you'd had the chance to study the hall closer," she said, "you might have found a photograph of a sandy-haired little boy with green eyes."

I frowned. "He was one of the children you rescued?"

"Not me," she said.

"Then who?"

She just looked at me.

"My father?"

She didn't answer. She didn't have to.

"My father rescued this guy?" I opened my mouth but no words came out. I closed it and then tried again. "But now he's my enemy?"

"He is," she said slowly, "worse than that."

"He set the fire. It nearly killed me."

Again she just stood there.

"Did he kill my father?"

"I don't know. You said he was there."

I nodded. "He was the paramedic."

"And he took away your father?"

"Yes."

She turned and looked at Spoon again. "That is all I know."

"What are you talking about?" I could hear the anger in my voice. "The first time I saw you, you stepped outside and told me point-blank that my father was alive. Don't you remember?"

She nodded. "I do," she said softly.

"Well, if you didn't know, why did you say that?"

She closed her eyes. "When I heard about your father's car accident, I cried. We get used to death and costs. I've explained that to you before. But your father had saved so many. Your mother too. They dedicated their lives to our cause and angered many bad people. But still, when I first heard about your father, I believed that it was just a tragic accident. I had no idea that Luther was involved."

"Luther?" I said. "That's his name?"

She took the photograph from my hand. "I should have known better, Mickey. Accidents happen, of course, but with people like us, odds are that there is something more nefarious at work. I was wrong."

"What made you change your mind?" I asked.

She looked at me.

"What made you suspect this Luther guy was involved?"

The old lady smiled, and for a second, I could see the child that she once was. "You don't believe in magic, do you, Mickey?"

Oh, please, I thought. "No."

"Neither do I. I've seen too much suffering to believe in the superstitious. And yet . . ."

I waited. When she didn't speak again, I tried a new avenue. "Who is this Luther? What's his last name?"

"I don't know."

"How can you not know?"

She shrugged. "We worry about the rescue, not the name."

"But my father rescued him?"

"Yes."

"And then you thought—"

"That your father died in a car accident."

"So what made you change your mind?" I asked again.

"You won't believe it. I don't believe it either. And yet I know what I know. I don't believe in magic or superstition. But I believe that there are some things we cannot yet comprehend—that there are things beyond our capabilities to understand. Sometimes, explaining how the universe works is like teaching a lion to read. Reading is real. The lion is real. But he's never going to read."

I shook off the analogy and yet I got it. "So what happened?" I asked.

"My refrigerator broke."

"Huh?"

"It's an old refrigerator," she said. "It hums so loudly. But I've had it a long time. I like it. Even the noise comforts me."

I tried not to sigh.

"Miss Sobek?"

"Lizzy."

"Pardon?"

"Call me Lizzy."

"Okay, great. Lizzy, I was asking about this Luther guy and my father."

"And I'm telling you. You need to be patient, Mickey."

I said nothing.

"Where was I?"

"You loved your loud refrigerator," I said, trying to keep the sarcasm out of my voice.

"Oh, right. Thank you. Yes, my refrigerator. I've had it since, oh, I don't know. Many, many years."

"Fascinating," I said, because I couldn't help it.

Lizzy ignored it. "One day, the refrigerator broke, so I called the repairman. This was, oh, I don't know. Maybe two months ago."

"Okay," I said, just to keep her moving along.

"So he said that he would come between noon and five P.M. That's how they do it, these repairmen. They don't give you a specific time, like they used to. They give you a block of time. You're supposed to sit and wait, but then again, I had no place to go."

I wanted to pull the words out of her mouth, but I guess that she needed to go at her own pace.

"So anyway, at noon I came downstairs. I like to sit in the living room and listen to my old record player. I play it all day long. I know it's funny for an old lady, but I love the old rock. The Who. The Rolling Stones. I have *Pet Sounds* by the Beach Boys. Have you ever heard it?"

"Yes."

"Do you like it?"

"Very much."

"Me too. My favorite is HorsePower. Do you know them?" I nodded. "They're my mother's favorite."

"I know." She smiled at me again. "But on that day, I wanted to be sure to hear the doorbell. I didn't want to miss the repairman. So I kept the music off. I made myself a cup of Earl Grey tea and sat at the kitchen table and waited for the repairman to arrive. It seemed to take forever."

"I know the feeling," I muttered.

"What?"

"Never mind. You were waiting for the repairman."

"Yes. And I fell asleep. Right there. Right at the kitchen table. I don't know why. I never nap during the day. But I was tired, I guess. Or maybe it was because the refrigerator was silent. Or that there was no music playing. I can't explain, but I fell asleep. And that's when I heard it."

"Heard what?"

"In my sleep. In my dream, I guess. I heard your father's voice."

I tried not to make a face. "In a dream?"

"Maybe."

"And, uh, what did he say?"

"I couldn't hear much. It was very muffled. But I knew it was his voice. I could make out the word *Luther.* That was about it. He sounded in trouble, though. There was panic in his voice. A knock on the door woke me up. The repairman was there."

I couldn't believe what I was hearing. "And this is why you thought my father was alive?"

"Yes."

"Because you heard a voice?"

"His voice."

"In your sleep?"

"Yes."

I didn't even know what to say to that.

"Mickey?"

"Yes."

"You know about the fate of my family, of course. My mother. My father. My beloved brother."

I nodded.

"They are all dead," she said. "So I know."

"Know what?"

"I know," she said, her voice a low cackle, "that the dead never speak to me."

Somewhere, way in the background, I heard hospital machines beeping.

"Not once," she went on. "All those deaths, all those years, all those ghosts. But they never speak to me. You want to roll your eyes at the old lady hearing voices? I understand that too. But as I've learned, we can't explain everything. Not yet anyway. I know what I heard. I heard your father. I heard him warn me about Luther."

I just sat there.

"And now Luther is back, isn't he? So maybe, just maybe, I'm not so crazy."

Silence. For a few moments we just stayed there, not moving. Finally I spoke.

"Is that why you Photoshopped his head on that Nazi picture?" I asked.

"Trick photography. Yes."

"You wanted to see my reaction? To see if I knew Luther?"

"Yes."

"Did you think that, what, I was working with him?"

"I didn't know. But he was there. You said that he took your father away."

"He did," I said. "But Dad rescued Luther, right?"

"Yes."

"So why would this Luther guy want to hurt him?"

"Things go wrong, Mickey." She looked at Spoon. The implication was obvious. "Just because you do right doesn't mean that wrong won't still find you."

I felt a tear in my eye. "So what do I do now?"

"You're already doing it. You have your assignment."

"What, you mean this guy Ema met online?"

"Yes."

"Why?"

"She will need to discover the truth. You have to help her."

"Okay."

"And, Mickey? We don't always make the rescue."

"What do you mean?"

"Your search. It may not end well."

"Why do you—?"

The door behind us opened. As the nurse started to come in, Lizzy Sobek moved with a speed that defied her age. She blew through the door, muttering an excuse-me to the confused nurse, and vanished down the corridor. I started toward it, but the nurse blocked my exit.

"Excuse me," she said to me, "but who was that?"

"Just another nurse," I said, and pushed past her.

When I reached the corridor, I looked left, then right. Nothing.

The Bat Lady was gone.

CHAPTER 17

The next day, Ema and I were at our usual outcast lunch table. I was about to fill her in on Bat Lady's visit when I saw Ema's eyes widen and leave mine.

"What?"

Ema didn't reply. She was looking over my shoulder, and judging from the expression on her face, some horror movie zombie was slowly approaching me from behind, ready to pounce and sink his teeth into my flesh.

I slowly turned to see what had caused Ema's terror.

Troy Taylor was walking toward us.

He carried an overloaded lunch tray. Three cartons of milk, a sandwich the size of a throw pillow, a heaping pile of French fries, Jell-O, I don't even want to know what else. He walked with an ease and confidence that Ema and I would never have in this room.

"What the . . . ?" Ema whispered. "He's not planning on—"

Troy stopped in front of us. He flashed a smile that almost made me reach for sunglasses and said, "Hey, mind if I sit with you guys?"

Before we could overcome our surprise enough to reply, Troy dropped his tray with a heavy thud and pulled out a chair. He sat as though someone had cut his legs out from under him. Then he picked up his sandwich with both hands.

"So how are you guys doing?"

He took a huge bite and started to chew.

Ema looked at him as though he'd just dropped out of a horse's behind. "What do you want?"

"Who said I want something?"

"Well, you don't normally sit here."

"I'm trying to broaden my horizons. Is that a problem?"

"You usually sit over there," Ema said, pointing at the "cool" table. "If you even so much as glance over here, it's usually to moo at me."

Troy put down his sandwich, wiped his hands on a napkin, and gave Ema the most solemn look I had ever seen on a teenager. "I wanted to apologize for that."

"Excuse me?"

"No, Ema—can I call you Ema? Or do you prefer Emma?"

Caught off guard, she said, "Uh, Ema is fine."

"Great, thanks. No, Ema, it is I who needs to be excused, not you. I was wrong."

"You were wrong every day?" Ema asked. "Every day since, oh, sixth grade or so?"

"I was, yes. I was horrible. I have nothing to say in my defense. Sure, I could blame Buck. You know that he was the leader of all that kind of stuff. Maybe I felt peer pressure, I don't know. You might think it's easy being at that table, being—yeah, I know how this sounds—one of the kings. But like Mrs. Friedman taught us in European History, 'Uneasy lies the head that wears the crown.'"

Ema and I sat there, mouths agape.

"So maybe it's because Buck is gone now," Troy continued. "Maybe recent events are making me see things more clearly. But really, Ema, I want to apologize and try to start anew."

"You're kidding, right?"

Troy looked wounded. "I've never been more serious."

"You must think I'm an idiot."

"How so?"

"You're a user, Troy."

"Ema," I said.

Her head snapped toward me. "What? You're buying this?"

"No, but—"

"You're being used, Mickey. He's not here because he's had some great epiphany or because Buck is gone. He's here because he wants us to help him get off for failing a drug test."

"Ema?"

It was Troy. She slowly turned her head toward him.

"You may be right," he said.

"What?"

"I'm not claiming Mickey and I are going to be best friends," he went on, "but we're teammates. It's a bond that's hard to understand. We both want to win—and we want to win with our teammates by our side."

"You did it, Troy. We both know you're guilty."

"Then the last thing I'd want to do is keep the whole mess front and center, right?" Troy said. "If I was guilty, I'd stay quiet. That's what my old man wants me to do."

That quieted Ema for a moment.

"I understand how you feel," Troy said.

"No, you don't," Ema said. "How would you have reacted if I'd sat at your table? You'd probably start mooing or something."

"That's a good question," he said with a nod. "It hurts to hear. But it's a fair point."

"So you fail a drug test and now you want us to believe that you've seen the light?"

Troy thought about it. "The truth is, I need Mickey's help. You have no idea how hard that was to admit. Brandon really helped me see that. And, yeah, I know how this sounds, but maybe talking to Mickey, you know, face-to-face and all, maybe that's what it was. It's easy to hate at a distance. It's not so easy to hate face-to-face, like this."

Ema just frowned.

"But when I was talking to Mickey, I started thinking about everything. My whole life, I guess. Here was some guy I've been a total jerk to and he's willing to help me. I'd have never done that. I'm being honest here. It made me think. It made me wonder about what kind of guy I am and what kind of guy I want to be. I took a long, hard look at myself. I don't think I've ever done that before. Things have always come easy to me. Maybe I needed this, I don't know. Either way, I took a long, hard look in the mirror—and I didn't like what I saw."

Troy stood and picked up his tray. "I don't blame you, Ema. And I don't expect to make amends in one day. Tiny steps. So if you won't accept my apologies for all the horrible things I've said over the years—and you shouldn't yet—please accept my apologies for barging in on you guys like this." He gave me a nod and started on his way. "See you around."

I almost called out to him, but I let it go. Ema didn't reply either. She just lowered her head and started picking at her food.

"He's full of it, you know."

I didn't say anything. I didn't blame her. I got it. I more than got it. I didn't fully trust him either, and I had only been subjected to his bullying for a few weeks. Ema had dealt with it most of her life.

At the same time, he had come to us. He had made the first move. I hated the idea of merely rejecting him back. It felt wrong. It felt like something they would do, not us.

Ema put down her fork. "We should look into Troy's drug test."

"Really?"

Ema nodded. "So we can prove once and for all that he's a lying bully."

CHAPTER 18

After school I received a group text from Spoon. It was addressed to Rachel, Ema, and me.

Got something. Stop by tonight?

We all texted back that we would.

I got to the locker room early, changed, and found my way to the basket in the corner. I was the first one there and I enjoyed five minutes of solitude. The next guy out of the locker room was a junior named Danny Brown. As I saw him grab a basketball and stroll onto the court, I stopped dribbling and waited for the customary stony glare.

Only I didn't get one.

More than that, instead of heading toward the center basket, Danny Brown started making his way toward me.

"Hey, Mickey," he said.

"Uh, hey, Danny."

No one had ever introduced us. We had never exchanged words before. But that was how it was. Other guys came out, and again, to my astonishment, they made their way toward my corner basket. Danny grabbed the rebound and threw it out to me. We ran passing and shooting drills. People said hello to me. They slapped me five. They asked how I was liking the new school. They asked about some of my classes. They warned me about teachers to stay away from and offered me study guides that would be helpful.

One guy, a senior named Eric Bachmann, asked me if I needed a ride home after practice.

For the first time in my life, I felt I was part of a team.

I know that sounds like nothing in comparison to what was going on around me. Ema had a missing boyfriend. I had a dead father and a mom in rehab, and this crazy Luther guy was probably after me. But right now, for just a minute or two, I let myself revel in this wonderful camaraderie that came so easily to others.

The joy continued on the court. My teammates passed to me. I passed to them. On one fast break, I faked a drive to the hoop, hoisted the ball up over my head, and as though we had communicated telepathically, Brandon leapt high in the air, grabbed the ball in one hand, and sailed in for the alley-oop slam dunk.

Basketball can be poetry in motion.

Everyone whooped and hollered and slapped my back.

Brandon just pointed to me, gave a little nod, and started back on defense.

I can't tell you how good that felt.

The cheerleaders were practicing in the corner. They had all seen the play. Rachel gave me a small smile, and my heart did a backflip.

Practice on the court was only an hour today. The second hour was weightlifting down the street at Schultz's Health Club. The club was all sleek machines and chrome weights. Television screens adorned the cardio machines. There was a small clothing store and a juice bar. The music was loud and pulsating.

But our moods sobered up the moment we entered the gym. Schultz's was owned by Boris Schultz, Buck's father, and coming here made everyone think of him. Twenty-plus years ago, Mr. Schultz had been a big-time bodybuilder, a former Mr. New Jersey who reached the top ten for Mr. America. He was still huge with a chest big enough to play paddleball on. He sported a severe crew cut. He looked like the kind of angles and hard edges where if you bumped into him, you could break a bone.

Today, though, Mr. Schultz somehow looked smaller. I had seen that before in my mother and maybe in myself. Illness can do that to you, but so could sadness. He led us through our weightlifting stations, trying to sound upbeat and enthusiastic but today it felt flat. Chest press, bicep curls, squats. He yelled out all the usual encouraging clichés about maximizing effort and "come on, two more" and stuff like that.

But his heart wasn't in it.

The last time we had been here, no one had wanted to partner up with me. Coach Stashower had finally stepped forward and gone through the circuit as my partner. Today I had plenty of volunteers and ended up with Danny Brown. We were about halfway through the circuit when I spotted something peculiar. Or should I say, someone.

Uncle Myron?

I could see him standing in Mr. Schultz's office through the big glass window. Mr. Schultz left the weight area and greeted him. Buck's older brother, town legend Randy Schultz, was also there. Someone had once explained to me the odds of becoming a professional athlete. In short, they are close to zero. Kasselton is a pretty big town. I read somewhere that in our New Jersey county, for every three thousand boys who start playing organized basketball in third grade, only one will eventually play college on some level—Division One, Two, or Three. So think about it. In our town alone, the league started with five hundred kids. That meant one kid every six years would play any college basketball on any level. The odds of going pro from there?

Forget it.

In the history of the sports-crazy town of Kasselton, there had only been one professional athlete out of the thousands of kids who'd participated, though injuries prevented him from playing more than a game or two.

You guessed it. Uncle Myron Bolitar.

Now, for the first time since Myron's career came crashing down two decades ago, Kasselton had another potential professional athlete—a football tight end named Randy Schultz, Buck's older brother. After breaking every receiving record at Kasselton High, Randy had gone on to stardom in the Big Ten, was named MVP of the Orange Bowl, and was currently waiting for the NFL draft. The experts had Randy pegged to go somewhere in the first two rounds.

Kasselton was poised to have its first professional football player.

But right now Randy Schultz, future professional tight end, looked grim and serious—and he was talking to my uncle. The conversation was animated, at least on Randy's part. I looked over, trying to catch Myron's eyes. Buck's father spotted me. He frowned and pulled down the shade.

What was that all about?

"Mickey?"

It was Danny Brown.

"Next station."

The squat rack. I loaded on the weight and spotted Danny. We finished up and headed back to the locker room.

"A couple of us are going to hang out at Pizzaiola after practice. You want a ride? I can take you home afterward."

A flush of joy rushed through me. "Uh, sure, thanks."

He gave me a crooked smile. I showered and tried to suppress the smile. It had been a good day. There had been painfully few in the past eight months. I wanted one night of being normal. I wanted a night where I could go out for pizza with my teammates.

Was that so wrong?

Ten guys ended up at Pizzaiola. I would tell you what we talked about, but it was just guy talk. We complained about the local pro teams. We poked gentle fun at some of the teachers. We talked about girls, though I didn't really know any of them. They asked me questions about myself.

"Where did you live before this?"

"Lots of places," I said.

"Like?"

"Africa mostly. South America, Asia, Europe. We traveled a lot."

They listened wide-eyed. Most of them had only lived and known life in Kasselton. The second "newest" player had moved to town eight years ago. These guys had all grown up together. They knew everything about one another, could almost predict what the other would say, knew exactly how to make one another laugh, what buttons to push, when to back off.

For these guys, I had turned from weird to exotic.

I don't know how much pizza we ate, but it was a lot. Brandon especially could put it away. Adults came in and said hello and asked about the team's chances. Everyone seemed to know everyone. Brandon always stood and shook the adult's hand. Sometimes he would introduce them to us with too much polish. "Mr. Mignone, allow me to introduce you to" and then he'd name us from right to left. Most of the guys nodded back. I hadn't been raised that way, so I too stood and shook each hand. Inevitably they would say the same thing:

"'Bolitar'? Are you related to Myron?"

"I'm his nephew."

They would put together then that I was Brad's son and grow quiet.

Like I said, everyone knew everyone. I guessed, at some point, that meant they knew my dad too.

I was having fun, especially when the attention turned away from me and they let me just observe and listen. I laughed a lot. I tried to remember the last time I laughed this much, and I don't think I ever had. I wanted the world to go away. I wanted to forget about the Abeona Shelter or missing kids or my dad or . . .

Or Spoon in that hospital bed.

I closed my eyes. Yeah, I wanted to forget. Just for one night. But I didn't get that. I got a few hours, and maybe, for now, that was enough.

My phone buzzed when the text came in. It was from Ema:

we're all here. where are you????

CHAPTER 19

When I arrived at the hospital, Ema and Rachel met me by the elevator. Ema looked at me warily.

"What time did practice end?" she asked.

"Don't worry about it."

Rachel could see the tension, but she wisely let it go. "Come on. We can all go in."

"I thought it was only one of us at a time."

"New nurse, new rule," Rachel said. "Today's said it was okay."

Rachel led the way. I fell in behind her with Ema, who kept her eyes focused straight ahead.

"What?" I asked her.

"It's late."

"So?"

"So where were you?"

"Basketball."

"That ended hours ago," Ema said.

"You're kidding, right?"

Ema kept walking.

"I have to report in to you wherever I'm going?"

"Only when you say you're going to meet me."

"I lost track of time. I had practice and we went to Buck's dad's gym and then, I don't know, we went to Pizzaiola."

She stopped. "You went with *them* for pizza?"

"Them. They're my teammates, Ema. Don't you get that?"

She just shook her head.

"What now?"

"You don't get it, do you?" she said.

"They're my teammates. I don't have to hate them."

"I didn't say you had to."

"But?"

"But nothing, Mickey. You're free to do whatever you want."

"Thanks, Mom," I said.

We reached Spoon's room. He sat up in bed with that wonderful, dopey smile on his face. "Hey, Mickey, did you tell them?"

"Tell them what?"

"That I'm meant for great things."

"Wait," I said, "you heard that?"

"I heard *everything*."

"So the whole time Bat Lady was here . . ."

"I was awake, yep."

Rachel gasped. "She was here? In this room?"

Ema stared daggers at me. Great. Now that I got the basketball team to stop with the stares, Ema had picked up the habit.

"Yep," Spoon said. "She pretended to be a nurse. She said I was meant for great things." He wiggled his eyebrows at Rachel. "Impressed?"

I looked at Ema. "I was going to tell you at lunch," I said to her, "but then Troy came by . . ."

"That's okay," Rachel said, though I hadn't been talking to her. I think that she knew. I think that she was trying to save me. "So what did she say?"

I filled them in on the Bat Lady's visit. When I finished, Rachel said, "So now we know for certain. We have to find Jared Lowell."

I nodded. Ema didn't. She had stopped staring daggers. Now she just looked plain hurt. Part of me understood. Part of me was getting a little annoyed.

"The question is," Rachel continued, "how?"

Spoon cleared his throat. "That's where I come in."

We all turned to him. He clicked a button on his laptop. "I have just sent you all my most recent file on Jared Lowell. I managed to get into his Farnsworth School files. He's a good student, by the way. Top of his class. But more important, I got both his dorm address and course schedule. You'll also find a campus map in the attachment." Spoon pushed the glasses up his nose. "With this information, it shouldn't be hard to find him."

"The campus is in Connecticut," Rachel said.

"I know."

"So how are we going to get up there?"

"Oh," Spoon said, "Mickey drives."

"Not legally," Ema said.

"And I can't just drive up to Connecticut," I said. "It's wrong to do it locally, but it would be way too risky to go that far without a license. Plus my uncle has confiscated all the car keys."

"You could take the bus," Spoon said. He was typing on the laptop. "Let's see. Grab the four-four-one on Northfield Avenue and change in Newark." He listed some morning departure times. "You could take a taxi from there."

"So when do we go?" I asked.

"No school tomorrow," Ema said. "Teacher conference. It'll be our best chance."

I would need to be back by 4:00 P.M. for basketball practice, but I didn't feel the need to tell her that right now. A phone buzzed. It was Rachel's. She took a look at her screen and frowned. I couldn't help it. I wondered whether it was Troy.

"It's my dad," she said with a heavy sigh. "Ever since my mom died . . ."

She didn't finish the sentence. We all understood.

"He wants to know where I am," she said. "I better go."

Rachel pocketed her phone and hoisted up her backpack. "It'll be tough for me to get away tomorrow. Dad wants to take me out to breakfast and then maybe to visit my grandmother."

"You don't have to explain," I said.

"We can handle this," Ema added.

"Might need someone back here anyway," I said. "Just in case."

I had no idea what I meant by that, but it sounded good, like we were giving her something to do. But Ema was right. We didn't need three of us going up there anyway.

We said our good-byes and Rachel walked out the door. When she was gone, Spoon looked up at me and said, "We can work on two things at the same time, Mickey."

"Meaning?"

"Meaning Bat Lady talked to you about Luther."

I said nothing.

"Luther is the guy in that photograph you gave me, right?"

"Right."

"Your Butcher?" Ema asked.

I nodded.

"So your dad was like us," Spoon said. "He rescued kids for Abeona."

"Yes," I said.

"Did you know?"

"No," I said. "Or maybe I suspected, I don't know."

"I don't get it," Ema said. "If your father rescued Luther, why would he now be trying to hurt you?"

"Simple," Spoon said.

"How's that?"

"Luther must not have wanted to be rescued."

I looked at Ema. She looked at me.

"I don't understand."

"Neither do I yet," Spoon said. "But Bat Lady said sometimes things go wrong. I started to think about it. I remember reading about Stockholm syndrome. You know what that is?"

I had a vague idea, but I let him tell us.

"You start liking your captives. You don't know it's wrong anymore. Or I was reading about kids with really bad parents—parents who hurt them—but they still want to stay with them. So maybe this Luther was like that. Maybe Luther didn't want to be rescued."

I glanced at Ema. "He's making sense," she said.

Spoon spread his arms. "I'm just full of surprises, aren't I?"

"So how does that help us find him?"

"That's what I plan on finding out," Spoon said. "I got that picture you gave me. I got a first name. It isn't a lot, but maybe I'll find something."

CHAPTER 20

Ema was quiet in the elevator.

"Let's take the first bus up to Connecticut tomorrow," I said. "We could be up at Jared's school by ten."

"Okay," Ema said.

"What's wrong?"

"Nothing."

I frowned at her.

"I know how much you want to be part of that team," she said.

"And I know that scares you," I said.

"What?"

"You think I'll start hanging out with them instead of you?"

Ema shook her head. "You're so thick sometimes."

"That's not it?"

"No, that's not it."

We were outside now. The night air was cool, and I welcomed it. Hospital air is always stilted and heavy. It is hard to breathe in a hospital. I stopped a moment and sucked in a deep breath.

"Then what?" I asked.

"Never mind."

"Come on, don't be like that. What?"

"With some people, you tell them the oven is hot, they don't touch it," Ema said. "But other people have to touch the oven. They have to feel the pain."

I frowned again. "That's deep, Ema. And isn't it supposed to be a frying pan?"

She stopped and put her hands on my arms. I saw her eyes in the moonlight look up at me. We just stood there a second and a weird thought hit me:

I wanted to kiss her.

I don't think I ever consciously thought about that before. We had always been squarely in the "friend zone." But looking down on her in this wonderful light, I wanted to cup her face in my hands and kiss her.

"You're going to touch the oven," she said. "I want to protect you from that pain. But I can't. I can only tell you that when it hurts, I'll be there for you."

"And I'll be there for you," I said. "Always."

"Always," Ema repeated.

We stared into each other's eyes. I don't know how long. I was about to move my hands to her face when someone driving by us honked and yelled, "Get a room!"

That broke the spell.

Ema's hands slid off my arms. She took a step back. We both turned and started for home. We walked in silence for a while. Neither of us would raise this. We would both just pretend the moment never happened. With each step it seemed farther away, as though we were leaving the near kiss in the hospital parking lot. The tension eased.

We were becoming just friends again.

When we reached the intersection, Ema surprised me by starting down the road toward Bat Lady's now-burned-down house. I stayed right by her side.

"What are you thinking?" I asked.

"There are tunnels under the house. That's what you told me."

"Right."

"And last time we went down to the basement, we found a clue."

"You're thinking maybe we can find another?"

Ema shrugged. "It's worth a try."

I had thought the same thing, of course. It was dark out now. It would be easier to approach without being seen by neighbors. Then again, the night also made an already spooky place even spookier. We stopped on the sidewalk.

Up ahead of us, the house's collapsed remains stood in

menacing silhouette. The streetlights were dim. The house had been built right along the woods. It was odd, I thought now, how none of the trees behind it caught fire.

What horrors, I wondered, had this house seen over the years?

We didn't have flashlights on us, but we had our smartphones. I got the flashlight app ready. I didn't want to use it until we were belowground. A light might be seen by nosy neighbors. They'd call the police, and let's just say that wouldn't end well.

Our approach was blocked by dozens of signs reading KEEP OUT and NO TRESPASSING. The yellow tape wrapped around the burned ruins worked like a reflector on a kid's bike.

"Strange," Ema whispered.

"What?"

"All the signs, the tape. It's almost overkill."

I had thought about that too. Were the police and fire department really that worried about keeping people out? The signs didn't look officially issued, just something you'd buy at the hardware store. I wondered whether Lizzy Sobek had put them up. I couldn't see that. Maybe it was one of the other people who worked for the Abeona Shelter. Maybe it was the guy with the shaved head whom I had recently learned was named Dylan Shaykes.

Didn't matter. I didn't care about the warnings. I was going in. There might be clues about Jared Lowell somewhere in the bowels of this property, but I was more thinking that there might be information about my father's sworn enemy, the mysterious Luther.

Bat Lady—sorry, I still thought of her that way rather than Lizzy Sobek—had said that Luther had been rescued by Abeona and that his photograph had been in that hallway he burned down to the ground.

"Another thing," Ema whispered.

"What?"

"Why did Luther set the house on fire?"

"Because I was in it."

It was too dark to see her face, but I could feel her skeptical frown. "So why not, I don't know, shoot or stab you? Why burn an entire house to the ground?"

I saw where she was going with this. "Because he wanted to destroy evidence."

"Could be."

"And some of the evidence—"

"Could be in those tunnels under the house," Ema finished for me.

We reached what had been the front stoop before the fire. I remembered how decrepit the house had been, how the very foundations seemed to shake when I knocked on that door, how the paint job was so old that flakes fell off as though it had a bad case of dandruff.

Now the house was rubble. But somehow that didn't seem to lessen the power. The fire had been put out days ago, but an acrid smell assaulted my senses. There was no smoke or smoldering going on, but it still seemed as though steam was coming up from the wreckage. I thought about what this house had held. I thought about the fact that a legendary hero from the Holocaust, long thought dead, had lived here in hiding for so many years. I thought about all the children who had been rescued, all the ones who had temporarily been hidden here or had healed here or had told their tales here.

The building might be gone, but those voices still whispered to us.

Ema took my hand as we stepped into the debris. We had been here before. We knew the way. The fireplace had been on the left. There had been an old photograph of Bat Lady with a group of hippies, probably taken in the sixties. I rescued that picture from the fire. It was in the drawer next to my bed.

Everything in the room was gone—the couch, the old record player where Bat Lady played her rock 'n' roll vinyl albums, the chair, the armoire, all of it. They were soot and dust.

I flicked on the flashlight app, keeping the beam low. Last time I'd been here, the basement stairs had been blocked by debris. They weren't now, but that was probably because I had made an opening.

I turned off the app. Okay, I knew where to go now.

I started toward it. Ema stayed with me.

"I'll go down first and make sure it's safe," I said.

"Because you're the big brave man?"

"Because I've been down there before, remember?"

"I do. You made me stay up here, remember?"

I sighed. "You want to go first?"

"And bruise your heroic ego? Not a chance."

I shook my head. The moonlight was just enough to catch her teasing smile. I wanted to give her a gentle shake. Or maybe kiss her.

Man, I had to stop thinking like this.

The opening was a giant hole. I shined the light down it for a brief moment. The stairs did not look sturdy enough to hold my weight, but I didn't have any choice. I knew the drop was not far anyway. I just had to be prepared.

When I reached the third step, I heard a cracking noise. I leapt right before the stair gave way and landed on the concrete floor.

"You okay?" Ema asked.

"Fine."

I turned on my flashlight app. I was below the earth now. The neighbors would not be able to see the beam.

"I'm coming down," Ema said.

"Wait."

"What?"

The beam of the flashlight danced around the room. In one corner, there was a washer and dryer that looked like something from the Eisenhower administration. Some old clothes were piled on the left. I opened two of the cardboard boxes. There was nothing but junk in them. No files, no clues, all a mess of dust and soot.

"Don't bother," I said. "There's nothing here."

"Are you sure?"

I checked the floor again. That was where I'd found the photograph last time we were here. But there was nothing now. Finally I raised the beam toward where I knew the answer would be.

The reinforced steel door.

I had seen it last time I was here. While everything else in this house had been decaying, this door was stronger than ever. I put my hand against it. The soot fell away and I could still see a shine. I tried the knob.

Locked.

I had expected that. I tried to push my shoulder against it. It didn't budge a bit.

I needed to get to the other side of that door.

But there was no way I was going to make it this way. That didn't mean I was defeated. I just had to go another route.

"Mickey?"

"I'm coming back up."

I tested the bottom steps. They were sturdy enough. I climbed a few. Ema lowered her hand to offer me help. I didn't need it, but if I refused it, she would make another crack about me being sexist or whatever. So I took it, which may have been an even more sexist move.

"So what now?" she asked when I was back aboveground.

"The garage," I said. "When Dylan Shaykes brought me here, he had me go through a tunnel that started in the garage out back and made its way to the house. I saw other corridors and doors. One, I bet, leads to whatever is behind that steel door."

The garage was in the woods, about fifty yards away. It seemed so odd, but then again everything about this property did. The woods came right up to the very house, as though they had sneaked in one night and taken over the backyard. That had made no sense to me. Now, of course, I understood it better. There was a road in the woods. You could drive up to the garage back there without fear of being seen. You could even use the tunnel in the garage and enter the house without anyone ever noticing.

There was a lot of secrecy surrounding the Abeona Shelter.

The garage doors were locked, but this time the doors weren't reinforced with anything. I checked the bolt and saw it was right by the knob. Good. I lifted my leg and smashed my heel into the spot directly above the knob.

The door gave way.

"So we're breaking and entering," Ema said.

"Probably."

She shrugged and headed in first. I aimed the flashlight at the ground and said, "Stop."

"What?"

I gestured toward the floor. There were fresh footprints in the dirt.

I put my foot next to one of the prints. I wear a size thirteen. This shoe was only slightly smaller, which meant that the prints probably belonged to an adult male.

Using my flashlight, I followed the footprints right up to the . . .

The trapdoor that led to the tunnel. They stopped there.

Never one to miss the obvious, I said, "Someone's been here recently."

"Or is still here now," Ema added.

Silence.

Then I said, "Let me—"

"If you say 'go down alone,' I will punch you."

I looked up at her. "Then neither of us goes down."

"Huh?"

"Spoon is paralyzed. He got shot. I'm not taking any more chances."

Ema shook her head. "We have to do this, Mickey. You know that."

"We don't have to do anything. Suppose Luther is down there."

"Then we have him cornered."

"You're kidding, right?"

Ema moved closer to me. "What else can we do, Mickey? Go home?"

I wanted her to go home. But I knew that she wouldn't.

"We'll be careful," she said. "Okay?"

What choice did I have? "Okay."

The trapdoor had a latch. I bent down and pulled the handle. We both looked down into the tunnel.

Darkness. Nothing but a black hole.

"Terrific," I said.

Ema had already turned on her flashlight app. There was a ladder leading down. She said, "Me first," and put her foot on the first rung.

"Let me go."

"I don't trust you. You'll look up my skirt."

"Uh, you're wearing jeans."

"Oops." She smothered a nervous laugh and started down the ladder. I followed. When we reached the bottom, Ema aimed the beam in front of her. The flashlight wasn't all that strong, but it just confirmed what I already knew: We were in a tunnel. At the end of it, if we made the proper turns, would be that steel-reinforced door.

The question was, what else would we find?

She was about to start forward when I put my hand on her arm. She turned toward me. I put a finger to my lips to signal for her to stay silent. She did so. I listened hard.

Nothing.

That was a good sign. Everything echoed down here. If Luther or someone else was moving, we would have heard them. Of course, that didn't mean that they weren't down here. The echo worked both ways. They would have heard us descending the ladder. Luther or whoever could be waiting somewhere, ducking low, ready to pounce.

"We move slowly," I whispered.

Ema nodded.

We started down the tunnel. I wondered how something

like this had been built. No way it passed Kasselton code. Did Lizzy Sobek hire construction workers? I doubted it. Did volunteers work on it? Did those "chosen" by the Abeona Shelter build this tunnel?

Maybe. Maybe my father helped build it.

But I somehow doubted it. It seemed older than that. How long did it take to construct? And really, who cared anyway?

We reached a door.

I remembered passing this door the last time I was here. Dylan Shaykes, who had brought me, told me to keep going. I tried to flash back and remember now. Did he seem afraid? No. He had just wanted me to keep going because I had been brought here to see Bat Lady.

I reached for the knob.

But there wasn't one.

Huh? I looked again. I could see what looked to be a keyhole. Nothing else. The door was smooth. It was also reinforced steel. I pushed against it. No yield at all.

What was Abeona trying to hide?

We were about to continue along the corridor when Ema said, "Mickey, look."

I turned to Ema. At first I didn't see it, but then I followed the flashlight beam down toward the ground. There was a small lever, like something you'd pull for a fire alarm.

"What do you think?" I asked her.

"I think we pull it."

Ema reached for it before I could. Her hand took hold and

pulled. At first, it didn't give at all. Then she pulled harder. The lever gave way with a sucking pop sound.

The wall next to us started to slide.

We stepped back and watched it move. It was bizarre. The front part of the wall came forward and moved to the right. It slid in front of the steel-reinforced door, covering it.

Ema said, "What the . . . ?"

The door was gone now. Completely camouflaged.

We stood there for a moment and stared, half expecting something else to happen. It didn't. The door was gone. I wondered whether there were more doors in this tunnel.

Or more levers.

"Pull it again," I said.

She did. The wall grunted before moving back to where it had been before. The door was once again visible. I pushed on the door one more time, hoping that maybe the lever unlocked it or something, but it didn't give.

"I don't get it," I said.

"Neither do I. Should we keep moving?"

I nodded. There wasn't much more for us to do here.

There was a fork up ahead in the tunnel. We stopped at it. I tried to remember when I was here last which way I went. I didn't remember the fork but I was pretty distracted. Dylan Shaykes—at that time I only thought of him as Shaved Head—was leading me toward the house.

What way had we gone—left or right?

Right, I thought. I don't have a great sense of direction, but right also seemed the way to the house. Plus, the bigger prong in the fork—the one you would more naturally take—was the one on the right.

I had already gone in that direction, though, hadn't I?

I was about to shine the flashlight to the left when I heard a noise. I froze.

Ema whispered, "What?"

"Did you hear that?"

"I don't think so."

We stayed still. I heard it again. I couldn't tell what it was, though. My imagination? Maybe. But whatever it was, it seemed very far away. Have you ever had that? Have you ever heard a sound so soft, so far away, so muffled that you aren't even sure that you are hearing anything at all? Like maybe your ears are ringing and you're just imagining the whole thing.

That was what this was like.

"Do you hear it?" I asked her.

And again, because we are so much in tune, Ema replied, "Maybe. Something really faint . . ."

We didn't know what to do.

"It could just be an old pipe," Ema said. "Or house noises. You know. You can barely hear it at all."

"I know."

"So what should we do?"

"Probably not stay much longer."

I shone the flashlight to my left. When we both saw what was there, Ema said, "Bingo."

Maybe, I thought.

The first thing we saw was an old television set. I don't know how old exactly. I mean, it wasn't ancient—not like that noisy refrigerator that broke on the Bat Lady—but it was a thick console set with a screen that couldn't be more than eight inches. A machine that looked like a giant old-fashioned tape recorder was attached to it.

"It's for VCR tapes, I think," Ema said. "We still have something like it in the theater room."

I stepped into the room. On the shelf above, there were dozens of tapes, lined up like books. I started to pull them down from the shelf.

"I don't think they're for a VCR," I said.

Uncle Myron had old VCR tapes of his high school games in the house. These tapes looked slightly different. They were a little smaller, less rectangular. I hoped to find something on the labels, but the only thing written on them were numbers.

"Mickey?"

It was Ema. Her tone made my blood go cold. I turned slowly toward her. Ema's eyes were wide. Her hand was resting on top of the television.

"What's the matter?" I asked.

"The television," she said.

"What about it?"

I saw her swallow. "It's warm," she said. "Someone was just using it."

We both froze again, in this dark, dank space, and listened.

Another noise. This one was real. No mistaking it.

Ema looked down at the attached tape machine. She pressed a button and a tape ejected from the machine. She jammed it into her purse and said, "Let's get out of here."

I didn't argue. We hurried back into the tunnel, this time heading toward the garage. We had gone about ten yards when I heard the noise behind me. I stopped and turned to look back.

Luther was there.

He stood at the far end of the tunnel, glaring at us. For a moment, none of us moved. Even down here, even in this faint light, I could still see the sandy hair and green eyes. I flashed back to the first time I had seen them—the day of the car accident. I was lying injured, woozy, not sure what had happened. I looked to the side and saw my father lying very still. A paramedic looked back at me and shook his head.

That paramedic was down at the end of the tunnel.

Luther's hands formed two fists. He looked enraged. When he took a step toward us, Ema grabbed my arm and yelled, "Run!"

I didn't move.

He took another step.

Ema said, "Mickey?"

"Go," I said to her.

"What?"

"Go!" I shouted.

I wasn't leaving. I wasn't letting him escape again. This Luther, this man I didn't know, was my father's sworn enemy. That made him mine.

My father's grave might not have held any answers. But I bet this guy did.

I wasn't going to let him out of my sight again.

Luther and I faced each other like two gunslingers in an old Western movie. I wasn't sure what move to make. I had spent most of my life overseas, in a variety of countries, and my father had insisted that I learn the various martial arts. I was big. I was strong. I knew how to fight.

But most martial arts work by using your opponent's aggression. I had never learned, for example, how to sprint toward an opponent in a tunnel and take him down. I knew better how to counter an attack like that, how to roll with my adversary and incapacitate him.

So I waited another second for him to come toward me.

He waited too.

I wondered whether he knew how to fight. It didn't matter. He was not getting out of here. He was not getting near Ema. It was just the two of us.

No reason to wait any longer.

I started to calculate the distance and figure an angle of attack—go low, take out the legs—when I heard a voice behind us.

"What the—?"

Someone was coming down via the trapdoor in the garage. I thought maybe I recognized the voice.

"Kasselton police! Everybody freeze!"

It was Chief Taylor, Troy's father. He hurried down the ladder. I glanced for a second, no more. I kept my eyes on Luther's. He kept his eyes on me. But I turned away just for a second.

"For the love of . . ." Chief Taylor's mouth dropped open as he looked around in disbelief at the tunnel. "What is this place?"

Another officer was coming down the ladder behind him. I quickly turned back to Luther.

Luther started to run the other way.

"No!" I shouted.

"Freeze!" It was Chief Taylor again. The beam of his flashlight was on me. "Mickey Bolitar! Freeze right now!"

I didn't listen. I sprinted toward the end of the tunnel. When I veered right, I saw the door—the steel-reinforced one in the basement, maybe?—slam closed.

Luther had run through it.

I ran toward it. I put my hand on the knob.

"Okay, Mickey," Chief Taylor said, standing side by side with another officer, "that's far enough."

They were there. I had my hand on the knob and tried to calculate how long it would take to open the door and run through it. Too long. Taylor and the other officer would be on me.

That was when we all heard the scream.

The two police officers turned toward it.

"Help! Oh, help!"

Suddenly I got it. The scream and call for help had come from Ema, but I could tell, from the exaggerated tone, she wasn't in real danger.

Genius that she was, Ema was intentionally diverting their attention from me!

I didn't wait. I pulled open the door and ran through it. I was back in the basement. It was darker now. I heard a crunching noise above me. I used my flashlight app and shone it upward.

I saw Luther's leg on the top step.

I ran and leapt toward it. I grabbed the ankle and hung on for all I was worth. I was actually suspended in the air, my grip on his ankle loosening, when I felt his other foot stomp on my arm. I didn't care. I hung on.

"Let go of me!" Luther shouted.

"Where's my father?"

"He's dead!"

I didn't believe him. And I had a plan.

If I could just swing my legs to the stairs, I would have enough leverage to pull Luther down to the concrete basement floor.

"Let go of me!"

"No!"

I pulled and arched my back, aiming my legs for the stairs. Behind me I heard the door open.

"Freeze!"

It was Chief Taylor again.

"He's getting away!" I shouted.

But Chief Taylor and the other officer wouldn't listen. They tackled me instead. I tried to hold on, tried with everything I had to keep my grip, but I could feel my fingers slip away under their combined weight.

"He killed my father!"

I crashed to the ground. Above me, I saw Luther smile and slip away.

"Stay put," Taylor yelled.

"He killed my father! Stop him!"

"What are you talking about?"

But it was pointless. We were belowground. Luther was already off and running. Chief Taylor stood. The other officer flipped me onto my stomach and snapped the cuffs on me.

Ema came through the door. "Leave him alone! He didn't do anything!"

"You're both under arrest," Taylor said.

"For what?"

"A neighbor saw you break into the garage. That's a crime. You've wiggled out of plenty of trouble, Mickey, but not this time."

"Listen to me," I said, "you have to find that man."

"I don't have to find anyone," Chief Taylor said. "I told you to stop. You didn't. You ran away from a police officer. You resisted arrest. I'm sorry, Mickey. You've gotten too many breaks."

Ema tried. "But if you'd just listen to us—"

Chief Taylor spun toward her. "Do you want me to cuff you too, missy?"

"What?"

"Turn around."

"You're kidding—"

"Turn around!"

Ema did so. I watched in disbelief as Chief Taylor cuffed her too.

"I don't want to hear another word out of either of you."

They led us back down the corridor through the tunnel. Again I saw Taylor looking around as though he couldn't believe his eyes. "What is this place?" he asked me.

I said nothing.

"I asked you a question, Mickey."

"I don't know."

"So why did you break into the garage?"

"I don't know what you're talking about."

I saw his face redden. "That's it. I've had enough of you. I'm taking you down to the city prison in Newark. You're going to spend some time in that system. Adult population. I told you once about the guy with the really long fingernails, remember? You're about to be his cellmate. Jackson?"

He turned to the other officer.

"Let's lock them in the squad car and check out this tunnel."

It was hard to get us up the ladder because our hands were cuffed behind our backs. Jackson suggested taking them off us. Taylor refused. When we reached the front yard, he said, "You wait with them here. I'm going back into—"

"What's going on here?"

We all stopped at the sound of the scratchy old voice. There, standing on the sidewalk as though she had just materialized, was Bat Lady. Jackson choked back a scream. Bat Lady was back in her full crazy-person persona—the long white-to-yellow gown, ratty slippers, her white hair flowing down to her waist.

"Ma'am," Taylor said, risking a step in her direction, "these two broke into your own garage."

"No, they didn't."

"Uh, yes, ma'am, we spotted—"

"Don't 'yes, ma'am' me," she snapped. "They have permission to be here. I asked them to check my tunnel for me."

"You did?"

"Of course."

"Well, about that tunnel—"

"Why are they handcuffed?"

"Well, see, we got a report that they broke in—"

"And I just told you that they did no such thing, didn't I?" She waited for an answer.

"Uh, yes, ma'am."

"So uncuff those children immediately."

Taylor gestured at Jackson. Jackson took out a key.

"Ma'am, could you tell what those tunnels are for?"

"No."

"Pardon?"

"Do you have a warrant?"

"A warrant? No. Like I said, we got a report—"

"Has this become a police state? I've lived in police states before. They are horrible places."

"No, ma'am, this isn't a police state."

"Then you have no right to be on my property, do you?"

"We were responding to a call."

"Which was made in error obviously. So now you know that. Do you know what I want you to do now?"

"Um . . ." I was enjoying watching Chief Taylor squirm. "Leave?"

"Exactly. Don't make me ask again. Shoo."

CHAPTER 21

After Chief Taylor's squad car drove off, Bat Lady started toward the garage. We followed her. I asked her questions. She didn't respond. Ema asked her questions. She didn't respond. She just kept walking in silence.

The woods seemed to be thicker now. The darkness settled over us like a blanket.

"Miss Sobek?" I tried again.

Finally she spoke. "Why did you come?"

"To find clues."

"About?"

"About Luther."

I couldn't see her in the dark. "I guess you found more than that."

"Who is he?"

"I told you."

"He said my father's dead."

The old woman didn't reply.

"Was he lying?"

"I told you before."

"You heard his voice."

"Yes."

"And the dead never talk to you."

She didn't bother replying.

Ema asked, "Are we going back to the tunnel?"

"No, Ema," Bat Lady said. "We will never go back there again."

"I don't understand."

"It's been exposed. The police know about it now."

"It was hardly a secret," I said. "Luther knew about it."

"Of course he did."

"I don't understand," Ema said. "Where are we going?"

"You're both going home."

"And you?"

She raised a hand straight in the air. Suddenly headlights came on. A car came up the road hidden in the woods. I wasn't surprised when I saw it. It was the same black car that had tailed me since I moved in with Uncle Myron. The passenger door opened.

Shaved Head stepped out. He was dressed, as always, in a black suit. Even at night, he still wore the sunglasses.

"Hello, Dylan," I said to him.

He ignored me.

"Go home," Bat Lady said to us. "Don't ever come back here."

"What are we supposed to do?" I asked.

"I told you already. You remember, don't you?"

I nodded. "You want us to find Jared Lowell."

Bat Lady looked at Ema as though she were seeing her for the first time. She stepped toward her and put her hands on her shoulders. "You're stronger than you know, Ema."

Ema glanced at me and then back at Bat Lady. "Uh, thanks."

"You love this boy."

"Well, I don't know about that. In a way I don't even know him."

"It will hurt."

"What will?" Ema asked.

"The truth."

Ema and I stood perfectly still.

"Go home. Both of you. Don't ever come back here."

Lizzy Sobek looked over her property as though seeing it for the first time—or, more likely, the last. I wondered what she saw, how much history lay on these grounds, how many rescued and terrified children had come through here.

"None of us," she said, "should ever come back."

Bat Lady seemed to float toward the car. Shaved Head/ Dylan opened the back door of the car. She slipped inside without another word. Dylan got into the front passenger seat.

The black car drove off.

CHAPTER 22

That night I dreamed about my mother.

I don't remember the specifics. The dream was pretty surreal. Mom was young in the dream, really young, like before-I-remember-her young. Sometimes my dream mom was wearing tennis whites. Other times not. She was healthy, though, smiling the way she used to, the way she did before my dad died and the demons moved in and took her away from me.

Why did she have Dad cremated and not tell me?

I didn't have a clue.

Why would she bury an urn of ashes as though it were his body? Again no clue. But I had seen the authorization form. That was her signature.

Or was it?

I had already been dumb enough to be fooled via common

Photoshopping that Luther was an old Nazi from World War II. Maybe the answer here was just as simple. Maybe Mom hadn't signed the document. Maybe someone had simply forged her name.

Again the obvious question: Why?

Answer: Take it a step at a time. See if Mom signed the papers. If she didn't, then we check on the notary. We see where that leads. But first things first.

I needed to see my mom.

"You're up early," Uncle Myron said a little too cheerfully.

"I'm going somewhere with Ema."

"Where?"

I didn't want to get into my trip to the Farnsworth School. "Just somewhere."

He didn't like it, but he didn't push it either. Uncle Myron was eating a bowl of unhealthy kid cereal and reading the back of the box. He did this every morning.

"Can I pour you some?"

He also asked this every morning. I'd rather just pour sugar down my throat. "No, thanks. I'll scramble up some eggs."

"I can do it for you."

He also made this offer every morning. Once I let him make them. They were terrible. Myron couldn't cook. He has trouble reheating a pizza without messing it up.

"I'm good, thanks."

I broke the eggs, added a dash of milk. Uncle Myron had

purchased some truffle oil for me. That was a secret I had learned from my mother. It was expensive, but when I could get it, a dab of the oil made the eggs a lot tastier.

"I need to see my mom," I said.

Uncle Myron looked up from the cereal box. "You can't."

"I know she's in rehab."

"And you know the doctors said we had to stay away for at least two more weeks."

"It's important."

Myron stood. "You want to ask her about the cremation."

"Right."

"It won't help," he said. "I mean, think about it. What's she going to tell you, Mickey?"

I stayed silent.

"If your mom says she didn't do it, maybe she was just so high she doesn't remember. If she says she did it . . ." Myron stopped, thought about it. "Well, okay, maybe that would end whatever quest you're on."

"I'm going to call the rehab," I said. "But I'm going to need you to back me up on this."

Uncle Myron let loose a long sigh but he nodded. "Okay, sure. But we need to do what's best for your mom. You get that, right?"

Of course I got that. He sat back down and started eating the kid cereal again. I moved to the stove. I had forty minutes until I was meeting Ema at the bus station. Then I remembered something.

"Hey, Myron?"

"What?"

"I saw you at Schultz's gym. You were talking to Mr. Schultz and Randy."

Myron took another bite of cereal. He may have nodded, I wasn't sure.

"What was that all about?" I asked.

"I've known the family for a long time. Mr. Schultz grew up in this town."

"Did he go to Kasselton High?"

"Yep."

"Your year?"

"No," Myron said. "Your father's."

I wasn't sure how to take that. "Did they know each other?"

"Your father and Mr. Schultz? Sure. They knew each other since grade school."

I tried to imagine that—a world where Buck's father and my father played at recess or whatever as little kids. It was hard to see. "So yesterday you were talking to him and Randy."

"Right."

"What about?"

He took another spoonful of cereal, jammed it into his mouth, chewed too loudly for all the time it had sat in milk. "Do you know what I do for a living?"

"I thought you were retired," I said.

"Temporarily, yeah. I mean, I sold my business. But do you know what I used to do?"

"You were a sports agent, right?"

"Right."

I was using a wooden spatula to work my eggs.

"So that's why they wanted to see you?" I asked.

"Pardon?"

Was Uncle Myron being intentionally thick? "Did Randy want you to be his agent?"

Myron's words came out slowly. "I don't think so."

"What, then?"

"When I was training to become an agent, I went to law school."

I knew about that. After Myron's basketball career came to an abrupt end, he ended up at Harvard and became an attorney. "So?"

"So what people tell me is confidential."

"When you're acting as a lawyer."

"Right."

"So you're Randy's lawyer?"

"No."

"I don't get it, then."

Uncle Myron started fidgeting. "Why are you so interested?" he asked.

"No reason," I said, trying to sound nonchalant. Then: "Do you know he has a brother, Buck?"

"Yeah, I know. He's a senior. He's given you some trouble, right?"

"Not anymore."

Myron nodded. "Mr. Schultz told me. Buck moved back in with his mother. Something about a custody dispute. He was pretty upset about it."

"So was that what he wanted to talk to you about?" I asked.

"I'm not a divorce lawyer," Myron said.

"Is that a no?"

"It's a no."

I waited. Uncle Myron started reading the back of the cereal box closely now, as though it were religious scripture. "You're not going to tell me what you guys were talking about, are you?"

He didn't bother glancing up. "No, Mickey, I'm not."

"Could you tell me if it had anything to do with Buck?"

Uncle Myron weighed that request before saying, "It doesn't."

"So," I said, "the fact that Randy wanted to talk to you and Buck all of a sudden had to go live with his mom—that's just a big coincidence?"

"Yes," Myron said.

But I could hear in his tone that even he didn't believe it.

CHAPTER 23

I met Ema at the bus stop. "It isn't a VCR tape," she said.

"What is it, then?"

"Something called a Betamax. Sony made them. I guess they were popular in the eighties, but they're obsolete now."

"So how do we watch it?"

"I don't know. We could look online, I guess. See if anyone is selling a machine on eBay or something. Or we could go back to Bat Lady's house and use the one in the tunnel."

"You heard her."

Ema nodded. "Never go back. She was pretty adamant about that."

The bus hit some traffic near the Tappan Zee Bridge, but still made it in less than three hours. There were three Farnsworth students on our bus—all wearing jackets and ties—so we followed them. Campus was closer than we'd expected, less than a half-mile walk.

We stayed a step behind the three boys. Every once in a while they would turn around and look at us, wondering, I guess, why we were following them. Sometimes they stared openly at Ema. There may have been derision in their eyes, I couldn't say for sure. Ema was decked out in her customary black—black clothes, black hair, black nail polish, black lipstick. Tattoos ran up and down her arms and across her neck.

I could almost feel her growing uncomfortable next to me, so I decided to break the tension by speaking: "Hey, guys."

They all turned now and squinted at us.

"Do you know Jared Lowell?" I asked.

"Yeah, sure," one of them said. The kid had a big mop of blond hair. "Why, you guys friends?"

I looked at Ema. She looked at me. Man, I hadn't thought this through. "Uh, sort of."

Under her breath Ema muttered, "Smooth."

Blond Mop said, "What's that supposed to mean?"

"Nothing."

But now Blond Mop looked at me with suspicion. We passed a place called Wilke's Deli. A bunch of students were lined up to get lunch.

"Uh, I'm his cousin," I said lamely.

Ema looked on in horror.

"You are?"

"Yeah."

"I guess height runs in the family, then."

"I guess."

"If you're his cousin," Blond Mop said, "why did you say 'sort of' when I asked if you knew him?"

Ema folded her arms. She wanted to hear this too.

"Did I?" I fumbled. "Oh, I thought you asked if we were friends. We're cousins. That's 'sort of' friends. You know what I mean?" I smiled like the local TV anchorman. Up ahead I saw a tall white steeple that I recognized from the Farnsworth School website. We were getting close to campus. "Hey, nice meeting you."

We quickly veered right. Out of the side of her mouth, Ema said, "Wow, you're good."

"Thanks."

"I was being sarcastic."

"Yeah, me too."

She stopped. "Mickey?"

"What?"

"How do I look?"

"Great."

"Don't patronize me."

"I'm not."

Ema started to bite a nail.

"What's wrong?" I asked.

"I really care about this guy, okay? I know you want to dismiss it because it was online. But I have feelings for him. I miss him. We shared in a way that . . ."

I felt a small pang. I waited for her to continue. Then I said, "In a way that what?"

She shook her head. "Never mind. Let's go."

On the website, the campus looked beautiful; in person, it looked even better. The perfectly aged brick buildings lined the perimeter of an expansive circle of pure golf-tournament-green grass. The grass has been cut in perfect strips. The circle was big enough to house two soccer fields and a baseball diamond. The fields were all empty now, the entire campus still. I checked the clock on my phone and then I looked at the class schedule.

"Jared is in his Comparative Lit class," I said. "He gets out in twenty minutes."

"So what do we do in the meantime?"

I noticed two security guards standing in a booth. One of the guards stared at us. I realized how out of place Ema must look to him.

"We should probably get out of sight," I said. "It's an all-boys school, and, well, you probably stand out."

I meant her gender, of course, but it was more than that. This campus seemed pretty straitlaced and old-school. Ema looked anything but.

"Excuse me."

I had spoken a few seconds too late. The words had come from yet another campus security guard. He was a small man with a mustache so thick, it looked like someone had glued a guinea pig under his nose.

"Hi," I said.

"Are you a student here?" he asked me.

I was going to lie and say yes, but that wouldn't work. The guard would ask me for my student ID or look up my name or something like that. I was debating how to handle it when Ema enthusiastically stuck out her hand.

"Hi!" she said in this fake golly-gee voice that was nearly the polar opposite of her normal affect. "My name is Emma."

The guard hesitantly took her hand. "Uh, nice to meet you."

"And your name?" Ema asked, still holding the handshake.

"Bruce Bohuny."

"Well, nice to meet you too, Officer Bohuny! Oh, and this is my brother Mickey."

She gestured toward me. I nodded because I'm fast on the uptake.

"Say hi to Officer Bohuny, Mickey."

"Uh, hi."

Officer Bohuny and I shook hands.

Ema gave us both her biggest-wattage smile. Who was this girl? "Officer Bohuny, my brother is visiting the campus as a prospective student, and I thought I'd walk around with him. Is that a problem?"

"Well, see, you need visitor passes," he said.

"We do?" She frowned at me. "Mickey, did you know that?"

Me: "No. I didn't know."

"So you two don't have visitor passes?" Bohuny asked.

"I'm so, *so* sorry," Ema replied—and she looked more than sorry, almost crushed by this indiscretion. "What should we do, Officer Bohuny?"

"The admissions office is that building on the left." He pointed with both his finger and, it seemed, that bushy mustache. "The entrance is on the other side of the circle. You can get a pass there. I can walk you over there, if you'd like."

"Please don't bother," Ema said, shaking his hand again. "We've taken up enough of your time. Thank you so much, Officer Bohuny."

"Sure thing."

We started toward the admissions office. Officer Bohuny kept watch. Under my breath, I muttered to her, "Who are you?"

She gave a small laugh.

"Now what?" I asked.

"Keep walking."

"Do you have a plan?"

"I do," Ema said. "You're going to have to talk to Jared on your own."

"How?"

"We will go to the admissions. You tell them your name and that you're a prospective student interested in seeing the campus. You'll get a visitor's pass."

"What about you?"

She shook her head. "I can't play the sister card in there.

They might ask for ID. It will look too weird. You go on your own. Find Jared. I'll wait for you two at that deli we walked past."

Ema didn't hesitate or look behind her. She headed off campus while I continued to make my way to the admissions office. I had hoped to just get a pass and move on, but that was not about to happen. I had to fill out forms. I had to show my current ID. I had to schedule a campus tour at three o'clock and an interview at four.

"Would it be possible for me to walk around?" I asked when the paperwork was done. "I just want to experience the campus on my own a little."

The lady behind the desk frowned at me and then said, "Come with me a moment."

Uh-oh. I followed her down a wood-paneled corridor. Oil portraits of stern men, former headmasters, looked down on me disapprovingly. They seemed to say, "You don't belong here," and today, at least, it was hard to argue.

The receptionist stopped by a door and took a long look at me. "You're tall," she said.

I wasn't sure how to reply to that, so I didn't.

She opened the door and pulled out a blue blazer. "The school has a strict dress code. Didn't you read that in the literature?"

"I must have missed it," I said.

"Luckily you're wearing a collared shirt. Here's a tie."

I thanked her. The jacket was a little snug, but it would do. I threw the tie around my neck and began to tie it as we headed back to her desk. She gave me a visitor's pass and told me to wear it on my lapel. I did.

I checked the time. Jared's Comparative Lit class would be letting out in two minutes. I grabbed a more detailed campus map from the admissions office and tried not to hurry outside. Jared's class was in room 111, Feagles Hall. That was four buildings down on the right.

I hurried over, doing an awkward walk-run, and arrived with a few seconds to spare. The bell in the steeple chimed. I could hear the scuff of chairs on wood. The students started to exit. I leaned against the wall near room 111 and waited. Mr. Casual. Mr. Just Minding My Own Business.

Twelve boys exited the classroom. I had seen a picture of Jared Lowell. None of the faces matched. Jared had also been described as my height, but none of the students were over six feet tall. I still waited, still leaning against the wall as though I was holding it up, hoping that maybe he was just a straggler.

A few minutes later the teacher came out. By now the corridor was empty except for Mr. Casual. The teacher turned to me. "May I help you?"

I was going to ask him whether Jared Lowell had been to class, but I already knew the answer. If I asked where Jared was, well, hadn't I learned my lesson about asking questions haphazardly? I said no thank you and moved on my way.

Now what?

When I stepped outside, I was struck anew by how spectacular this campus was. How cool it must be to go to school here. The campus's green was one thing, but down the hill, the water sparkled in the sunlight. I wasn't sure what waterway that was—the Atlantic Ocean maybe?—but students were in crew boats rowing in perfect symmetry. The whole place felt upper class and rich. I expected a foxhunt or polo match to start up.

Maybe Jared was sick today. He lived, I knew thanks to Spoon, on the second floor of Barna House. I could go and see if he was there. The other option was to . . . to what? I could go find Ema at the deli, but then it might be harder to come back on campus without a lot of questions.

Might as well give it a try. I didn't see where there was much to lose.

Barna House had to be the newest building at Farnsworth. While the other buildings were all stately brick, this was sleek one-way glass. I tried the door. Locked. You needed a key card to get inside. I waited about ten seconds. A student opened the door from the inside. I smiled, held the door for him, and entered.

I'm a master at the art of the break-in.

Two boys were playing Ping-Pong on a Wii connected to a giant-screen TV. They still wore jackets and ties, though the ties were loosened to the point where they might serve better as belts. Groups of boys sat on either side of the combatants, cheering them on with a gusto I normally associated with live football games. There were oohs and ahhs and trash-talking.

I headed up to the second floor. I didn't know the room number, but as it turned out, I didn't need to. The names were right on the doors. I started down the corridor. I was surprised that all the rooms were singles. I had always pictured prep school students as having roommates.

The third door read JARED LOWELL and his graduation year. He was indeed a senior. I knocked on the door and waited.

"So who are you really?"

I turned to the voice. It was Blond Mop. He wore only a towel around his waist. The blond mop was wet and pasted to his forehead. I assumed that he had just gotten out of the shower.

He was waiting for my reply.

"My name is Mickey Bolitar. I'm looking for Jared. I don't mean him any harm."

"So why are you looking for him?"

"It's kind of a long story."

He just stood there dripping in his towel and waited.

"You saw my friend," I said.

"The goth girl?"

"Right. She's a friend of his. Online friend anyway. He suddenly stopped communicating. She was worried about him."

He frowned. "You came all this way for that?"

It did sound pretty lame, but I said, "Yes."

"And you came with her because . . . ?"

"She's my friend. I'm trying to help her."

He stood there in his towel, no shirt, water dripping off the mop of hair. "Is she some kind of a cyberstalker or something?"

"No. Look, I just need to see him and make sure he's okay."

"Just because he stopped texting her back or whatever?"

"There's more to it than that. But all I need to do is make sure he's okay."

"That's weird," the kid said. "You get that, right?"

"I do," I said.

He took a deep breath. This was surreal, talking to this preppy boy just standing there in his towel. "Do you play basketball?" he asked me.

You get this question a lot when you're six-four. "Yes."

"Me too. My name is Tristan Wanatick. I'm the point guard on the team here. Jared and I are co-captains. Seniors. It's our last year. We were supposed to have a great season."

I felt a small chill. "Supposed to?"

"We still will," Tristan said, trying to sound defiant but not quite getting there. "I mean, he said he'll be back."

"Jared?"

"Yeah."

"So he's not at school?"

Blond Mop shook his head.

"Where is he?" I asked.

"Something happened."

Another chill, bigger this time. "What?"

"I don't know. Some kind of family emergency. He left school a few days ago. Right in the middle of the semester. More than that—right at the start of basketball season."

"Where did he go?"

"Home."

"And you don't know why?"

"All I know is it was something sudden," he said. "But if Jared is missing basketball, it has to be something really, really bad."

CHAPTER 24

I promised Tristan I would let him know if I learned anything.

There was nothing more for us to do here. Ema and I caught the next bus back. I headed straight to school for basketball practice. It felt great, of course, to disappear in the sweat and strain and beauty. I sometimes wondered what my life would be without having the court as a place to escape.

When I got out, I was surprised to see a familiar car waiting for me.

Uncle Myron's.

He lowered the window. "Get in," he said.

"Something wrong?"

"You wanted to see your mother, right?"

"Right."

"Get in."

He didn't have to tell me twice. I circled around and hopped into the front passenger seat. Myron pulled away.

"How did you get permission?"

"You said it was important."

"It is."

Myron nodded. "I explained that to Christine."

Christine Shippee ran the Coddington Rehabilitation Center, where my mother was being treated for her addiction. Christine had told me in no uncertain terms that my mother would not be allowed any visitors, including her only child, for at least another two weeks.

"And she accepted that?" I asked.

"No. She said that you couldn't come."

"So how—?"

"Your mother isn't in jail, Mickey. She's in rehab. I told her that we were pulling her out of the program if she doesn't let you see her."

Whoa, I thought. "What did Christine say to that?"

I saw Myron's grip on the steering wheel tighten. "She said that we'd have to find your mother a new facility."

"What?"

"You said it was important."

"It is."

"So understand: Christine said that if we broke their protocol—if you saw her—then your mother would get thrown out."

I sat back.

"Well?" he asked.

"Well, what?"

"What do you want to do, Mickey? Do we go and see your mother right now? Or do we let her stay in the program and get the help she needs?"

I thought about it. He made the right turn and up ahead, not more than another mile, was the Coddington Rehabilitation Center.

"What do you want to do?" Myron asked again.

I turned toward him. "I want to see my mother."

"Even if that means getting her thrown out of the program?"

I sat back, crossed my arms, and said with more confidence than I really had: "Even if."

CHAPTER 25

"I don't understand this," Christine Shippee said.

"I just need to talk to her. It won't take long."

"She's going through withdrawal. You know what that is?"

"Yes."

"She's in tremendous pain. Her body is craving the drug. You have no idea how hard this part is on a person."

I had learned in life to compartmentalize. I understood what she was saying. More than that, I felt her words. Physically. I felt them like a hard blow to the stomach. But I had come to a horrible realization. This wasn't my mother's first stint in rehab. Kitty Bolitar, my mother, had gone through the pain of withdrawal before, just a few months ago. Kitty had convinced everybody that she was fine and then she had gotten out and smiled at me and taken me to school and promised to make me my favorite dinner with my favorite garlic bread and then I went to school and she went to a motel and shot that poison back into her veins.

That was why we were back here.

"It didn't work last time."

"That's not uncommon," Christine Shippee told me. "You know that."

"I do."

"Mickey, we are doing what's best for her. But I meant it. If you insist on seeing her tonight, you will break our protocol. We can no longer be her facility."

"I'm sorry to hear that."

Christine Shippee looked toward Myron. "He's a minor. This is your call, not his."

Uncle Myron turned to me and met my eye. I kept my gaze on him. "You're sure?" he asked me.

I was.

Christine Shippee shook her head. "You know where her room is," she said in a voice of both exhaustion and exasperation. "Myron, you can stay with me and sign the release papers."

She hit a button and I heard the familiar buzz of the door. I opened it and started down the narrow corridor. When I found my mother, she was asleep. Her ankles and wrists were restrained. Still, I felt somewhat lucky. I had caught her in a peaceful moment, deep sleep, escape from the pain.

For a few moments I stood in the doorway and watched her. She had given up her tennis career—the fame, the fortune, the passion, all of it—to keep me. She had loved me and taken care of me my whole life until . . . until she couldn't anymore. I have heard that the human spirit is indomitable, that it can't be beaten or destroyed, and if you want something bad enough, the human spirit is impossibly strong.

That's total crap.

My mother wasn't weak. My mother loved me with everything that she had. But sometimes a person can break, just like Bat Lady's stupid refrigerator. Sometimes they break and maybe they can't be fixed.

"Mickey?"

Kitty Bolitar smiled at me, and for a moment, her face beamed. She was my mom again. I ran over to the side of the bed, transformed suddenly into a little boy. I collapsed to my knees and lowered my head onto her shoulder and then I, too, broke down. I sobbed. I sobbed on her shoulder for a very long time. I could hear her making a gentle shushing sound, a sound she made for me a hundred times before, trying to comfort me. I waited for her to put her hand on my head, but the restraints wouldn't allow it.

"It's okay, Mickey. Shh, it's going to be okay."

But I didn't believe it. Worse, I didn't believe her.

I put myself together a piece at a time. When I could finally speak, I said, "I need to ask you something."

"What is it, sweetheart?"

I lifted my head. I wanted to look into her eyes when I asked. I wanted to see her reaction. "It's about Dad."

She winced. My parents loved each other. Oh, sure, right, lots of people's parents do. But not like this. Their love was embarrassing. Their love was complete and whole and the problem with that kind of love, the problem with two becoming one, is what happens when one dies?

By definition, so must the other.

"What about your father?" she asked.

"Why did you have him cremated?"

"What?" She sounded more confused than shocked.

"I saw the paper you signed. I'm not mad or anything. I get it. But I don't know why—"

"What are you talking about? He wasn't cremated."

"Yes, he was. You signed for it."

Her eyes blazed now, boring into mine. I don't think I had ever seen them this clear. "Mickey, listen to me. We buried your father in Los Angeles. I never had him cremated. Why would you think such a thing?"

She waited for the answer. I believed her. She hadn't been in a drug stupor or anything like that. I could see it in her face. And I could see something else in her face too.

We had all been pretending.

My mother wasn't going to get better. She was broken. Christine Shippee might be able to repair her for a little while, but she would just break again. There was only one hope for her. I knew that. When my father died, she died too. That was why I was willing to risk her treatment. That was why I didn't care about the threats to throw her out of rehab. Rehab wouldn't do any good. Right now, without my father, you were sticking a tiny bandage on a limb amputation.

My mother was lost to me forever. There was only one hope.

"Mom?"

"Yes."

I kept my tone strong. "I need you to get better."

"Oh, I will," she said, and, man, it sounded like a lie now.

"No, not like that. Not like last time. Things have changed."

"I don't understand, Mickey."

"Get better, Mom," I said, standing up now. "Because the next time I come back, I'm bringing Dad."

CHAPTER 26

I hurried out then. Christine Shippee said, "Wait, where are you going?"

"No," I said.

"What?"

I spun back to her. "She stays. I was only in there a few minutes. Please."

She looked at me, then at Myron. Myron shrugged.

"Please," I said again. "Just trust me, okay?"

Christine Shippee nodded. "Okay, but, Mickey?"

"Yes?"

"You can't do this again."

"Don't worry," I said. "I won't be back until everything has changed."

I was in school, on my way to practice the next day, when Rachel sent me a text: **In Philadelphia with my dad.**

I typed back: **Sounds like fun.**

I told him I knew the truth about my mom.

I nodded toward the screen. **How did it go?**

There was a small delay before she typed back: **Not well. Yet. But it chased the lie from the room.**

I smiled. **Good.**

Be back late tonight. Can you update me in the morning?

Sure.

Great. My place early AM. See you then. Take care.

I wrote back, because I'm the master of smooth: **You too.**

I stared down at the phone until a voice jarred me back to the present.

"What are you smiling at?"

I looked up too quickly. "Nothing."

Ema frowned. "Right."

"It was nothing. Someone just sent me a joke."

"One of your new jock friends? I bet it was a riot."

"What's up?"

"Guess who found us a Betamax machine so we can watch that tape," Ema said.

"You?"

"Nope. Spoon. If you can skip chilling with your hoops bros tonight, maybe we could go to the hospital and watch the tape together."

"I'm there," I said.

"Goodie."

Ema took off. I got ready for practice. A bunch of the guys

were joking around and I joined in and I enjoyed it and the heck with Ema and her attitude. I was allowed to have a little fun, wasn't I? I spotted Brandon lacing up his sneakers in the corner. He looked over at me and tilted his head as though asking, *Well?*

I walked over to him. "Let me ask you something," I said.

"What?"

"It's about Buck."

"What about him?"

"From what I understand, his parents are divorced."

"Right. I think they split three, four years ago, I don't know."

"Was it hard on Buck?"

Brandon squinted at me. "What difference does that make?"

"I'm just finding this all a little convenient."

"What?"

"Buck has lived his whole life in this town, right?"

"Right."

"So suddenly, a few weeks into his senior year, he has to leave his friends and school and live with his mother?"

Brandon shrugged. "I'm not a lawyer, but they have joint custody or something."

"So when was the last time you talked to him?"

"I don't know. A few days before he left."

"You haven't spoken to him since?"

"No."

"No text or e-mail, nothing?"

"A text, I think," Brandon said. "Maybe an e-mail."

"No good-bye?"

Brandon seemed to get it now. "No," he said. "No real good-bye."

"And you don't find that odd? You guys were friends from childhood. He moves away and never says good-bye?"

Still seated, Brandon looked up at me. "What are you getting at, Mickey?"

"The timing," I said.

Brandon said nothing.

"Look," I said, "I've only known Buck a short time. He's been nothing but this horrible bully. That's all I know of him. But I want to show you something."

"What?"

I started down the row of lockers into the hallway. Every high school has that sports trophy display case. I brought him over there and pointed to the photograph of last year's team on a plaque as county champions. I pointed at Buck.

"What?" Brandon said.

"You don't see it?"

"No. What is it?"

"Maybe because you saw him every day. I didn't. But take a good look at him."

"I am," Brandon said. He was very tall, so he bent down for a closer look. "What am I supposed to be seeing?"

"This picture was taken a year ago. It barely looks like the same Buck I know. This guy has to be thirty pounds smaller."

Brandon stayed hunched over and studied the photo. "So? Lots of guys grow between junior and senior year."

"That much?"

"Sure." But I could hear the doubt in his own voice. "Come to think of it . . ."

"What?"

"Buck had a great baseball season. The extra strength really made a difference in his slugging percentage . . ." Brandon's voice drifted off. Then he gave me a sharp look.

"What?" I said.

"You're supposed to be helping Troy."

"That's what I'm doing."

"It sounds more like you're trying to make a case against Buck."

"I'm not making a case for or against anyone. I'm trying to find out the truth. But suppose there's a connection between what happened to Buck and what happened to Troy."

"Like what?"

"I don't know yet. But suppose Buck got a positive drug test too. Wouldn't that maybe explain why he suddenly changed schools and doesn't communicate with anyone?"

Brandon looked off, considering it.

"What?" I said.

"It was always hard for Buck," Brandon said.

"How so?"

"The pressure on him. Being Randy's younger brother. It was more than just a shadow he couldn't escape. It was a shadow that smothered him. I know you hate him, and I can't say you don't have your reasons. But a lot of Buck's bullying behavior was because he always felt second best."

I arched an eyebrow. "His parents didn't hug him enough?"

"Hey, you're the one who raised this. But think about it. In the past few years, Buck has had to live with the superstar brother. That pressure had to be enormous."

I could feel my cheeks redden. "No, it didn't," I said.

"What?"

"That's an excuse." I tried to keep my breathing even, but Brandon took a step back. "My father had to live with a superstar brother too, remember?"

"I do."

Brandon looked at his feet.

"What?" I said.

"I don't mean to be cruel, Mickey, but how did that work out for him?"

His words landed right on my chin. "Low blow, Brandon."

"Not my intent," Brandon said.

"And my father didn't turn into a bully who called girls cows or threatened to beat up the new kid."

"No," Brandon said gently. "He didn't."

"I hear a but."

"Forget it."

"My father did good work. He helped the needy."

"And how about his relationship with his superstar brother?"

I couldn't believe that he was still going there. "When he

and his brother had their falling-out, Myron wasn't a superstar anymore. He'd already blown out his knee. Myron's career was over."

"You're right," Brandon said. But I could hear in his tone that he just wanted to move on. "Forget that. I'm not making excuses for Buck, but let's be real here. Buck was under a lot of pressure to perform, to live up to the hype of being Randy's brother. Then you add to that all the problems at home, his parents' divorce . . ."

"And his huge weight gains," I added.

"So I don't get it, Mickey. What are you trying to say?"

"I don't know. I just wonder if it's connected. Buck suddenly leaves town. Troy tests positive for steroids."

"I don't see how they're related."

"Neither do I," I said. Then I added: "Yet."

CHAPTER 27

When I stepped into Spoon's hospital room, Ema was already there. Mr. Spindel, Spoon's father and the school janitor, was up on a ladder, fiddling with wires behind the television.

"Almost done, Dad?" Spoon asked.

"I don't see why you need this here."

"I told you. Rachel has a copy of an old *Smurfs* show on Betamax. We all want to watch it."

Mr. Spindel stepped down from the ladder with a frown on his face. "That has to be the lamest lie I have ever heard."

"Or maybe," Spoon said, "it's something R rated and completely inappropriate."

Mr. Spindel sighed. "Sounds better than the Smurfs." He finished tightening the wire. "All yours," he said. He grabbed his stepladder and left the room.

I looked at the old machine. "Where did you get this?" I asked him.

"From home," Spoon said. "Where else?"

"You still have one?"

"Of course. While the Betamax had lost almost its entire market share to the VHS tape by 1988, Sony continued to manufacture them until 2002."

"Ooookay," I said.

Ema put the tape into the Betamax. She pressed the play button. I sat on the right front corner of the bed. Ema took the left. We left enough space between us for Spoon to see.

The hospital TV was mounted on the wall in front of us. Right now, the screen crackled in gray-and-white static. We waited. Ten seconds later, the picture cleared.

"Where is that?" Spoon asked.

Ema and I shared a glance. "That's the tunnel."

"The one under Bat Lady's house?"

"Yes," Ema said. "In fact, this is pretty close to where we found the tape."

"Cool beans," Spoon said.

The camera was pointed straight down the corridor, coming from a spot relatively close to the house and aiming at a spot more toward the garage. For ten seconds, nothing happened. Then the camera gave a little jerk and we heard a familiar voice say, "Oh, I'm so clumsy."

From behind the camera, Lizzy Sobek appeared.

She was wearing that long white gown, her gray hair down to her waist. She looked younger—it was hard to say how much—but her skin was less wrinkled. She turned back and looked at the camera. "Is it on, Dylan?"

Spoon said, "'Dylan'?"

"Dylan Shaykes," I said. "That's the name of the guy with the shaved head."

"The one who follows you in the black car?"

"Yes," I said.

"Why does that name ring a bell?" Spoon asked.

"From old milk cartons. He disappeared twenty-five years ago. There were a lot of stories on him recently—"

"And now he . . . ?"

"Works for the Abeona Shelter," I said.

"Like us."

"Shh," Ema said.

On the screen, Lizzy Sobek turned her back to the camera, spread her arms, and said, "Welcome."

We heard distant voices, but we couldn't see anything.

A voice from behind the camera, Dylan Shaykes's, said, "You're blocking me."

"Oh," Lizzy Sobek said. "Sorry."

She stepped to the side. I squinted at the screen. Four kids—or maybe it was five or six, hard to tell from the distance—appeared down the hall. They stumbled closer to the camera.

"You're safe now," Lizzy told them.

One of the kids stepped forward in a challenging way. He put his fists on his hips, almost Superman style. "Who are you? Why are we here?"

I heard Ema gasp. "Mickey?"

I nodded, unable to speak.

The boy looked to be about twelve years old. He moved closer to the camera—close enough that we could see that his hair was sandy blond. The picture quality wasn't good enough to see the green eyes, but I didn't need to know the color. The facial features were all the same. I would guess he was fifteen or twenty years younger, but there was no doubt in my mind.

It was Luther. My Butcher.

"We will explain everything to you in due time," Lizzy said.

But Luther was having none of it. "I want to know now."

The other children moved forward. One looked younger than Luther by maybe five years. The little boy was scared and confused. Luther threw his arm around him protectively.

"It's okay," Lizzy said in a gentle voice. "No one can ever hurt you again."

Another child, the one on the far right, started to cry. Lizzy moved toward him, her arms spread. He ran into her arms. She stroked his hair. The fourth child did the same. Lizzy took him in her grasp too.

"What the . . . ?" Ema asked.

"It's a rescue," Spoon said.

"Shh."

I stared at the screen. Still comforting the two children, Lizzy looked toward Luther and the other boy. Luther shook his head. His grip on the other boy tightened.

"It's okay," she said again.

A tear ran down Luther's cheek.

"You're safe here. No one will harm either of you."

From behind the camera, I heard Dylan say, "Uh-oh, I think we have company."

Lizzy turned toward him. I could see something like fear on her face. "Get them to the safe room. Hurry."

Then she turned back and said one word that made my whole world crumble anew:

"Brad?"

And then the voice, at once so familiar and yet so different: "I'm right here."

My teenage father stepped forward.

Ema said, "Oh my God. Is that . . . ?"

Tears were running freely down my face. I nodded.

"Get them fed and situated," Lizzy said to the teenager who would one day become my father.

"Yes, ma'am."

Lizzy, her face set, started back toward the camera. She walked past it and disappeared. For another second or two, I could see them all—the two children she had been comforting, Luther with his arm around the other scared boy, and my father. They all stood there, completely still, and then, with a snap, the screen went black.

CHAPTER 28

For a few moments, none of us moved. We just sat and stared at the TV screen.

"I have more information to use now," Spoon said. "Luther disappeared with three other boys approximately, what, twenty years ago. There has to be something about it on the web."

I nodded numbly. I did everything numbly. I could barely talk or think since we had watched the tape.

"Mickey?"

"Yeah, Spoon."

"We will find out what happened to your father, okay? I promise."

Look who was suddenly making the promises. I nodded. Numbly.

Ema took my hand. "Are you okay?"

Another numb nod. Then I said, "It's just . . ." I stopped

myself, but there I sat, Ema holding my hand, Spoon looking at me from his bed with such concern. "After my dad was killed, I didn't look at any pictures of him. You know? It just hurt too much. I don't know. I couldn't handle it."

"We understand," Ema said.

"Now I not only see him," I said, pointing toward the screen, "but I see him on a video made before I was even born. So it's just . . ."

No more words would come out.

"Totally get it," Spoon said.

"Absolutely," Ema added.

Ema and I were still holding hands. It felt good.

"Perhaps," Spoon said, "a distraction would be nice." He opened his laptop and started typing. "As you may remember, Jared Lowell lives on Adiona Island, off the coast of Massachusetts. It requires two buses and a ferry to get to. Since the only day in the next week where you don't have either school or basketball practice is tomorrow, I took the liberty of booking two tickets. You'll have to leave early again in the morning."

"Wait, I can't go tomorrow," Ema said. "I promised my mom I'd go to her show in New York."

"Maybe that's better," I said.

"What?"

"I can find Jared and talk to him without you there. Maybe he'll be more forthcoming."

Ema frowned. "You're kidding, right?"

"No, he's right," Spoon said. "Perhaps it is best you don't go."

"So Mickey goes alone?" Ema asked.

Then I remembered my texts with Rachel. "Not alone," I said. "I'll have backup."

CHAPTER 29

I admit that this action—coming all the way out to this island—seemed extreme.

Ema and I had already wasted half a day heading up to the Farnsworth School trying to find Jared Lowell. That was one thing. It made some sense. But now we stood on the ferry, watching Adiona Island grow larger as we approached, hoping against hope that maybe Jared was here and we would find him and this mystery would be over.

I shook my head thinking about it.

"What's wrong?" Rachel asked me.

The wind blew her hair across her face. I wanted to reach out and push it back, tuck it behind her ear, but of course, I didn't. "What are the odds he's even here?"

"Jared? He lives here, right?"

"Right."

"And that guy you met up at the prep school said he'd gone home, right?"

"Right."

"So I'd say the odds are pretty good."

I shook my head again.

"You don't agree?" she asked.

"Do you think we're going to just knock on his door and find him home?" I frowned. "It's never that easy for us."

Rachel smiled. "True."

But that was exactly what happened.

The ferry was loaded with two classes of people. The crowd on the top deck looked like they were going to a cricket match or an equestrian show. Some of the men had sweaters tied around their shoulders. Others wore tweed jackets. The women wore tennis skirts or summer dresses in loud pink and green. They spoke with jutted jaws and used the word *summer* as a verb. One guy wore an ascot. He called his wife "sassy." I thought it was a personality description, you know, like she was sassy, but after eavesdropping I realized that was her name. Sassy with a capital *S*.

The other class, on the deck below, were what I assumed were day workers or domestics. I had seen the same expressions, the same slumped shoulders on the bus going from Kasselton back to Newark. I didn't know much about Adiona Island, but judging by the ferry, it was a playground for the old-money jet-setter crowd.

When we got off the ferry, Rachel had the GPS app on her smartphone ready.

"The Lowells live on Discepolo Street," she said. "It's less than a mile from here. I guess we should walk."

It was a good guess, especially since there were no other options. There was nothing by the dock area. No taxis. No car rental. No restaurant or deli or even snack machine. Almost everyone else had cars at the dock. The lower deck hopped into the back of pickups. The upper tier had roadsters and antique cars and brands you normally associate with money.

In the distance we could see fancy homes along the water. They were big, of course, but not huge or new. They were more what one might call "stately" rather than some nouveau palace. Half a mile down the road we passed a ritzy tennis club, the kind where everyone wore only whites, like they were at Wimbledon or something.

No one else walked, so we got a few odd looks. Rachel, of course, got a few lingering glances, but she was used to that.

"How did it go with your father?" I asked.

"It'll be okay," she said.

"Are you mad at me?"

"For telling me about my mother?"

I nodded.

"No. I get it. My father thinks it was the wrong move. He thinks I'll feel guilty for the rest of my life."

"Is he right?"

Rachel shrugged. "I feel guilty now. I don't know how I'll feel tomorrow. But your uncle was right: I'd rather live with the guilt than the lie." She pointed up the hill. "We take that left."

When we did, we entered a whole different part of the island. If the island were also a ferry, we were now on the lower deck. Rather than lush trees, row houses now lined both sides of the streets. The plain brick and cookie-cutter architecture indicated that we were no longer among the hoity-toity. That was the thing with fancy islands for the rich. Someone had to work the electric and the water and the cable. Someone had to mow the expansive lawns and teach the tennis and clean the pools.

This eyesore of a street, tucked away where no one could really see it, was where these workers and all-year inhabitants lived.

"Are you sure we're on the right street?" I asked.

"I am," Rachel said. She pointed at one of the brick buildings. "It's that one—third on the left."

I shook my head. "Jared goes to an expensive prep school. That fits with this island."

"But it doesn't fit with this street," Rachel said.

"He plays basketball," I said. "It looks like he's very good."

"A scholarship kid?"

"Makes sense." We reached a cracked walkway made of concrete and started toward the door. "Now what?" I asked.

"We knock," Rachel said.

So we did—and Jared Lowell answered.

He was tall and good-looking, just like in the photographs. He wore a flannel shirt, jeans, and work boots. He looked at me first, then at Rachel. His eyes stayed on Rachel.

Big surprise.

A smile came to his lips.

"Can I help you?"

Rachel asked, "Are you Jared Lowell?"

"That's right. Who are you?"

"This is Mickey Bolitar," she said. He turned and gave me a brief though polite nod. "My name is Rachel Caldwell."

The names clearly didn't mean anything to him. From inside the house, I heard a woman's voice shout, "Jared? Who's there?"

"I got it, Ma."

"I didn't ask if you got it. I asked who's there."

Jared looked at us as though waiting for the answer. I said, "We're here on behalf of Ema Beaumont."

I wasn't sure what to suspect. The most likely answer to all of this remained the most obvious one: Ema had been catfished. This guy, this Jared, had no idea who she was or what we were talking about. Still, this visit would confirm that fact, and we could be on our way.

In another sense, our mission was over the moment Jared Lowell opened that door. Jared Lowell wasn't missing. We had found him. He was safe. The rest—whether he was the guy who'd befriended Ema online or not—was irrelevant.

So I expected him to say, "Who?" or "I don't know any Ema Beaumont" or something along those lines. But that was not what happened. Instead his face drained of all color.

"Jared?"

It was his mom again.

"Just some friends from town," he shouted back. "Everything's fine."

He stepped outside and closed the door behind him. He hurried down the cracked-concrete path. Rachel and I caught up to him.

"What are you doing here?" Jared asked.

"We're friends of Ema's," I said.

"So?"

"You know who she is, right?"

He didn't reply.

"Jared?"

"Yeah, I know who she is. So what?"

Jared looked at his front door as though expecting it to open. He picked up the pace. We kept up with him. When we reached the corner, he stopped abruptly.

"What's this about?" Jared asked me. "I got to get to work at the club soon."

Now that I had him in front of me, listening, I wasn't sure how to put it. "You, uh, had a relationship with her," I began.

"With Ema, you mean?"

"Yes."

He shrugged. "We communicated online, I guess."

"Just communicated?"

Jared looked over at Rachel, then back at me. "Why is this your business?"

Fair question.

Rachel said, "She's worried about you."

"Who?"

"Who do you think?" I snapped. "Ema."

"And how does any of this concern you two?"

"You were 'communicating'"—I made quote marks in the air—"online, right?"

"What if I was?"

"Well, Jared, you just stopped cold. Why?"

He shook his head slowly. "What's your name again? Never mind. This is really none of your business." He turned toward Rachel and his face softened. "No offense to you, Rachel, but I'm not sure it's your business either."

"Didn't forget *her* name," I mumbled.

"What?"

I stepped up to him. "You don't do that to a person," I said.

"Do what?"

"You don't just stop communicating with someone like that. You don't just disappear and not tell the other person. You don't just leave them hanging like that. It's mean."

"'It's mean'?" he repeated, turning toward Rachel. "Is he for real?"

"I agree with him," Rachel said.

That made him swallow. "Wait, I did send her an e-mail. Maybe, I don't know, maybe it got stuck in her spam folder or something."

"Yeah," I said in a voice dripping with sarcasm, "that seems likely."

There was a sound that drew his attention. I looked behind me to see what it was. The front door opened. A woman I assumed was his mother was standing in the doorway. "Everything okay, Jared?"

"Fine, Ma." Then in a quieter voice to us: "I have to go."

I stepped in his path. I didn't exactly block him, but the move definitely had some force behind it. "Wait a second," I said. "The two of us came a long way."

"For what?" he asked.

I looked at Rachel. She looked at me. I didn't have an answer. Jared Lowell wasn't missing. He wasn't in danger. He was, it seemed, a jerk, but that didn't make him in need of rescue.

"Why did you stop communicating with Ema?" I asked again.

"None of your business."

Again his eyes drifted toward Rachel, and when they did, a cold realization entered my brain.

"Oh man," I said.

"What?"

"When did you first see a picture of Ema?"

"What?"

A small seed of anger began to grow in my chest. "When did you first see what Ema looked like, Jared?"

He shrugged. "I don't remember."

"No?" I said. "So maybe—wild guess here—it was around the time you decided not to talk to her anymore?"

"I told you. We never talked."

"E-mailed, texted, whatever. You know what I mean. Is that when you first saw her picture?"

But I saw something churning behind his eyes. "Yeah? So what of it?" He grabbed my arm and pulled me away from Rachel. He spoke in a soft voice.

"Dude, do you really blame me? I mean, look at the girl you're with."

I was actually cocking my fist when I remembered that his mom was still at the front door.

"Jared?" she called out.

"I'll be there in a second, Ma." He leaned close to me and kept his voice low. "Look, okay, maybe I should have told her better. Maybe I should have made it clearer, but really, it wasn't a big thing."

"It was to her."

"That's not my problem."

"Yeah, Jared, it is."

"What? Are you going to hit me, big man? Defend Ema's honor?"

Man, I wanted to. I wanted to smack him good and hard. "You have no idea what a great person Ema is."

"Then why don't you date her?" He grinned. "I'd be happy to take Rachel off your hands."

Rachel put her hand on my shoulder, her way of telling me to stay calm. "Not worth it," she whispered.

"Look," Jared said, "I'll e-mail her, okay? I'll let her know. You're right about that. But, Mickey? You better get out of my face now, because one thing is for sure: This is none of your damned business."

CHAPTER 30

I called Ema, but it went straight into her voice mail. I sent her a brief text: **Found Jared. He's safe. Call if you have any questions.**

"I blew it," I said to Rachel.

"How?"

"Got too aggressive."

"You were mad."

"It's just . . . when I think of Ema waiting by her computer . . ."

Rachel smiled. "You're sweet."

I shook my head. "I didn't even ask him the important question."

"That being?"

"Why is Jared home? Why isn't he still at school?"

"We didn't come to change his life," Rachel said. "We were supposed to find him. Mission accomplished."

I knew that she was speaking the truth. Jared had vanished—and we had found him. Period. The end.

But something felt very wrong about it.

When we arrived back home, I got a text from Brandon Foley: **Anything new on Troy's test?**

I thought about it. I simply was not buying that Buck's mother would suddenly be granted full custody and that he would have to move away. Sure, I had heard of some pretty strange arrangements in cases of divorce, but who would move a kid when he was seventeen years old and already into his final year of high school?

It *might* make sense in a vacuum—if that was all that had happened. But at the same time Buck decided to leave, his best friend and cohort in crime, Troy Taylor, failed a drug test.

Coincidence?

I didn't think so. Troy insisted that he's innocent, and most of the guys on the team seemed to believe him. I started drawing little lines in my head, trying to make things connect.

My brain started to hurt.

I needed more information, so as soon as I made sure Rachel was home safe and sound, I decided that it was time I had a heart-to-heart with Troy.

I was going to text him, but I didn't have his number. I guessed that I could ask Brandon for it, but I was already in the neighborhood. One of the few things I had learned was that there is no substitute for face-to-face. No, I'm not going to bemoan the smartphones or how we all constantly text or check social media. It is what it is. But when you want information, when you want to see whether a person is telling the truth or lying, there is nothing better than to look them in the eye and watch their body language.

At least, that was what I thought.

When I arrived at Troy's door, I hesitated before knocking. I had been here before. Sort of. Rachel had "distracted" Troy—ugh—so that Ema and I could break into Chief Taylor's home office off the back kitchen. Ah, good times. Now I was knocking on his front door, like a real visitor.

Suppose Chief Taylor answered the door?

No "suppose" about it. Two seconds after I knocked, the door opened. Chief Taylor, still in full uniform, appeared. His eyes narrowed when he spotted me on the stoop. "Mickey Bolitar?"

"Hi, Chief Taylor," I said too cheerfully.

"What do you want?"

"Is, uh, Troy home?"

Chief Taylor frowned at me a few more seconds. Then he stepped aside and said, "Troy is in the basement."

"Thank you." I wiped my feet a few hundred times on the welcome mat and stepped into the house. He gestured toward a door across the room. I opened it and started down the steps.

"Troy?"

Nothing.

The room was dark and silent. I kept moving down the stairs. An eerie glow started providing some illumination. When I reached the bottom step, I saw what it was. A video game with plenty of blood and guts was playing on the big-screen television. I spotted Troy lounging on a gamer chair. Headphones covered his ears. His finger danced across the game controller.

He still didn't know I was here. He was lost in the game, shooting, dodging, changing weapons. I had never gotten into the video game craze because when we were overseas I didn't have access to it. When we first moved back to the United States earlier in the year, I had tried to play them, but I wasn't very good. Like anything else, video games took practice. I'd started playing too late, and maybe this was a weakness of my own, but I didn't like to do things I wasn't good at.

"Troy?"

He still didn't hear me. I touched him on the shoulder. He jumped up, eyes wide, as though ready to attack. When he saw it was me, confusion crossed his face for a split second, but it was quickly replaced with his ready smile.

"Hey, Mickey."

I didn't know what to think of this guy.

"Hey," I said. "I wanted to talk to you."

He took off the headphones and put the controller down.

"Have a seat."

I sat in the gamer chair next to him. It felt odd, sitting in this dark room, the television providing the only light. On the screen, the game characters continued on as though nothing had happened. They ran and shot and dived and hid.

"So what's up?" Troy asked.

"I need to ask you about Buck."

That seemed to surprise him. "What about him?"

"You two are close, right?"

"Best friends."

"Were you surprised when he moved away?"

"Surprised? I was more like shocked." Troy turned toward me a little more. "Why?"

"It's just odd," I said.

"What is?"

"You were close to Buck, so maybe you didn't see it. He put on a ton of size in the off-season."

"He was lifting hard," Troy said.

"That might be all it is, then."

Troy's eyes narrowed like his father's had upstairs. "But you don't think so?"

"I just wonder. He showed all the signs of steroid use. Increased size. He was nasty and aggressive. I heard he had a really good baseball season."

"Great season," Troy said. "He showed a lot of improvement."

"Too much improvement?" I asked.

Troy looked troubled by something.

"What?" I said.

"You think Buck may have been taking steroids."

"Yes."

"But what would that have to do with me?"

"I don't know. Maybe nothing."

Troy looked away.

"What is it?" I asked.

"Nothing."

"Troy, you asked for my help."

"I know. But I didn't want that help to come at the expense of a friend."

"That's not what I'm doing."

"No?"

"I'm trying to find out the truth here," I said. "That's all. So what's troubling you?"

Troy took a deep breath. "Buck felt threatened by you."

I leaned back. "Me?"

"Yes."

"Why?"

"Look, we treated you wrong. I told you that."

"What does that have to do with Buck?"

Troy started fiddling with the controller in his hand. "I think one reason we gave you so much flack was because, well, we know how good a player you are."

I said nothing.

"The five of us had been starters on the basketball team forever. But one of us was about to lose his starting position to you. It wouldn't have been Brandon, the center, or me, the point guard—"

He didn't finish the thought. I finished it for him.

"It would have been Buck."

Troy nodded. "Think about it. You know all the pressure he was already under with his brother being a superstar, right?"

"Yes."

"Now add you in the equation. It got to him. Bad. To lose your starting job in your last year . . ."

I saw where Troy was going with this. "So you think he took steroids."

"I'm not saying that. He's my friend. But at some point, Brandon and I wanted to lay off you. We knew that you could help us win. That's all that really mattered to me." He leaned closer to me. "But, see, I would still be a starter. Buck was the one on the fringe."

We sat there, in the dark, and watched the video game characters run rampant.

"He hasn't called me back," Troy said.

"Buck?"

"Yeah. He sent me a few texts, but he won't talk to me."

"Why do you think that is?"

Troy shrugged. "I don't know."

My cell phone rang. It was Ema. I got myself out of the chair and headed over to a quiet corner. "Hello?"

"You found Jared?"

"Yeah," I said. "Where are you?"

"We just got back home."

"I'm on my way."

CHAPTER 31

I told Ema everything about our meeting on Adiona Island with Jared Lowell.

She listened intently, as she always did. We were sitting in the kitchen of the enormous mansion she calls home. Niles, the family butler, was puttering around the house, but he knew better than to get in our way. Ema's mom, the actress whose fan board had started this whole thing, was still in New York.

When I finished, Ema didn't speak. She just sat at the kitchen table. Her hands were folded in front of her. She stared at them. I started to reach my hand across, but I stopped. Her body language was all wrong.

"Ema?" I said.

"He's lying."

I waited for her to say more. She kept her eyes on her hands. She started twisting the silver skull ring on her right hand around and around. Finally she said, "I want to show you something."

She took out her smartphone and started playing with the buttons. I sat quietly. "I don't like doing this," she said.

"Doing what?"

"Showing you this e-mail. It's the last one Jared sent me."

"You don't have to . . ."

"I know that. And, yeah, it's really personal. That's why I don't really want to do it. But I need you to understand. Okay?"

"Yeah, okay."

With a deep sigh, Ema handed me her phone. The cover was black with silver studs. The girl was consistent, I had to say that. She had blown up the screen so I couldn't see the address or the top of the e-mail. I didn't scroll. If she had wanted me to see the whole thing, she would have left it alone.

I can't wait to see you. I can't wait for this all to be over
and to tell you what's in my heart and how I've changed.
You changed me, Ema. I have made so many mistakes and
there is still one more thing to do, but once that's over,
I promise it will all be behind me. We will be together if
you'll accept me.

I looked up. "That's it?"

"That's all I want to show you."

"What's with the 'if you'll accept me'?" I asked.

"I don't know."

I handed her back the phone.

"But does that sound like a guy who had a change of heart?"

"No, but you know how guys are."

"I do," Ema said with a frown.

I thought about it. "Jared wrote that he still has one more thing to do and then he can put it all behind him. What was he talking about?"

"I don't know."

I mulled it over for a few seconds. "He left school. Do you think it has to do with that?"

"I guess it has to," Ema said. "School was important to him. He's as basketball crazy as you are." She checked her phone and slid it back into her pocket. "Did he tell you why he was home?"

"No."

"Did you ask?"

"No."

"Why not?"

I remembered what Rachel had said. "We didn't come to change his life. Our mission was to find him and make sure he was safe."

My words came out with more sting than I intended. This all felt strange for some reason. Seeing that e-mail had thrown me off guard a little. Ema, a girl I cared about a whole lot, had this big relationship with some guy she was really into and with whom she exchanged words of . . . love?

I wanted not to care. But I didn't like it.

For a second—a half second, maybe less—I considered asking her when she had first sent him her picture. Had it been late in the game, maybe right after she received this e-mail? I know how cruel that sounded, but I had seen the way Jared looked at Rachel.

Was that it? Was the answer that simple—and that superficial?

I started thinking about that again and now my emotions turned back to rage at Jared Lowell.

But I stayed quiet.

"He may still be in danger," Ema said. "He could be covering something up. He could be trying to protect me."

"Protect you how?"

"There was something going on in his life. Something he was trying to get away from so that he could be with me. But suppose he couldn't? Suppose he tried to but, whatever it was, he couldn't escape it."

We sat there in silence. Finally I asked, "What was he trying to escape?"

"I don't know," she said. "But maybe we still need to find out."

CHAPTER 32

It was dark when I headed home. Niles offered me a ride, but I wanted to walk. I needed to clear my head. The walk home would do me good. Ema's house was not only ginormous but it sat atop a ginormous plot of land. I started down a driveway that had to be a quarter mile long.

When I reached the bottom of the hill, I spotted the familiar car across the street. It was black with tinted windows. Its license plate number was A30432. During the Holocaust, prisoners in Auschwitz had numbers tattooed on their arms. Lizzy Sobek had survived that death camp. Her tattoo number?

A30432.

The car was here for me. I didn't walk toward it. I would let them make the first move.

The back door opened. The man I had called Shaved Head stepped out. He wore a dark suit and tie. I knew now that his name was Dylan Shaykes. As a young child, curly-haired Dylan Shaykes had vanished, never to be seen again. I didn't know what happened or how he had joined Abeona, but he had been watching me from the beginning.

The black car drove away, leaving Dylan alone on the street with me.

"Funny thing," I called to him.

"What?"

"I've never seen the driver. Who is he?"

Dylan didn't answer. I didn't expect him to. "Let's take a walk," he said.

We started down the street together. Neither of us spoke for the first hundred yards or so. We were waiting each other out. It was odd. I had always thought my . . . what was he anyway? My mentor? My immediate superior? I didn't know. But I always thought that my relationship with a guy like this would be more teacher-student, master-pupil, like in some karate movie. But it wasn't. He was on my side. I knew that. He had been with Abeona a long time and would, I'm sure, help me in a pinch, yet there was always a tension between us.

"You have something that doesn't belong to you," Dylan said.

"What's that?"

"A tape."

"Oh, right. Well, since my father was on it, I kinda think it belongs to me too."

We kept walking.

"My father helped rescue Luther, didn't he?"

"Yes."

"So why is Luther our enemy now?"

"It's a long story," Dylan said.

"I can walk slower if you'd like."

"You're still new to this," Dylan said.

"Not that new."

"Do you know who Abeona was?"

"A Roman goddess who protected children."

"Something like that," Dylan said. "To be more exact, Abeona is the Roman goddess of outward journeys. She guards over children as they leave their home for the first time to explore the world."

"Okay," I said. "And how long has the Abeona Shelter existed?"

He smiled. "No one knows."

"What does that mean?"

"I was called. You were called. Lizzy Sobek was called. There were ones called before her. There will be ones called after us."

"And you don't know when it all started?"

"No."

"Who calls us?"

"For now? It's Lizzy Sobek. One day, we will have a new leader." He smiled at me. "I have been on both ends, Mickey. I'm a rescuer. And I was rescued."

I flashed back to the "memorial" service for a little boy named Dylan Shaykes. "Everyone thinks you're dead."

He kept walking.

"Even your father."

"Yes."

"You're okay with that?"

"He's the reason I was rescued. My father . . ." He closed his eyes for a second, as though in pain. "He was a cruel man."

"Did Bat Lady rescue you?"

"Her name is Lizzy Sobek."

"I know. But it's dangerous to use her real name, right?"

He nodded. "Good point. Yes. She rescued me. I was in the hospital. My father had hurt me. Again. I told the police that I fell down the stairs. Again. I don't think they believed me, but my father could be a very charming man when he wanted to be. I remember sitting in the hospital room and thinking about hurting myself again. So I could stay longer. I didn't want to go back to that house. I was scared." He stroked his chin. "Do you know those containers for disposable needles?"

I nodded.

"I tried to break into it. So I could get a needle. I thought maybe I could use it as a weapon or . . ."

"Or what?" I asked.

"Or I could use it to kill myself."

There may have been sounds around us. There may have

been cars driving by or children playing somewhere nearby or something like that. But I heard none of it.

"Bat Lady came in. She was dressed like a nurse. She took me away."

"Where did she take you?"

A small smile came to his lips. "Where do you think?"

I remembered the tape he wanted. "To that tunnel?"

"Yes. For a long time, that was where we hid the rescued until we could find them safe transport. There is a door down there. It can be hidden by a false wall."

"I saw it," I said.

"When you found that tape?"

I remembered it now. I had walked past it. "Yes."

"Anyway, that's where I stayed for the first two weeks. There was so much attention that they couldn't move me. The room has all this canned food and a toilet and a shower. It's soundproof so if, say, a scared child started crying, the police or a nosy visitor wouldn't hear. Two other boys were down there with me too. One was already there when I arrived. One came a few days later. Eventually we were moved."

"Moved where?"

"Someplace safe. We never find out where they go. That's part of how Abeona works. We compartmentalize. So I don't know what happened to those boys."

"And you?"

"In my case, I was sent to England. I grew up in the town of Bristol."

That explained the accent. This all made sense. No one knew about that tunnel. You could approach it hidden, from the woods and into the garage. "I blew it, I guess."

"Pardon?"

"You can't use that secret room anymore," I said. "Now I understand what Bat Lady meant. The police know about it now. If more kids go missing, it will be the first place they look."

"True," he said. "But the house is gone anyway. We had been using the tunnel. But that secret room . . ." A shadow crossed his face. "We stopped using that room a long time ago."

"I don't understand."

"We sealed it shut. It hasn't been open in years."

"Why?"

Dylan didn't answer right away.

"Why did you stop using that room?"

"That's what I need you to understand, Mickey."

"What?"

"You watched the tape with Luther and your father?"

It felt as though a cold hand had caressed the back of my neck. "Yes."

"Those boys were the last ones to ever use that secret room."

CHAPTER 33

Dylan started walking faster.

"Wait," I called to him. "What happened?"

"We rescued a little girl once. I won't tell you the horrors she had to endure. Her mother had done things to her that would boggle the imagination. But the little girl still thought that woman was her mother. She didn't know any better. She thought that she loved this evil woman. That's what happens. You get attached to your abuser, especially when you're a young child who doesn't know any better."

Spoon had said something like this. Something about Stockholm syndrome. I remembered how defiant Luther had been on the tape.

"And that was the case with Luther?"

"Yes."

"So what happened?"

"Your father made a mistake that night."

"What kind of mistake?"

"Someone had seen him."

Again I thought about what we had seen when we watched the video in Spoon's room. There had been a sudden interruption. "They followed him back to the house," I said.

"Yes."

"That's when you all started panicking. I saw it on the tape."

Dylan nodded.

"So who was it?"

"The state police."

"Did they search the house?"

"Yes."

"But they didn't find the boys."

"No. They were in the secret room. We had the false wall covering the door. Luther was calling for help."

"But the police couldn't hear him."

Dylan looked pained again. "Exactly."

"So what happened?" I asked.

"You noticed the smaller boy on the tape. The one Luther had his arm around?"

"Yes."

"His name was Ricky."

Was. He said "was."

"He wasn't Luther's biological or even adopted brother.

But in most ways, Ricky meant more to Luther than that. Those two had gone through hell and back together. Luther had always protected him."

"What happened to him?"

Dylan took a breath and let it go. "He died."

I felt my throat clench. "How?"

"You have to understand. The police were watching us. They even brought Lizzy Sobek to the police station to ask her questions. We have a powerful lawyer on the Abeona team. She came and helped us get through it. But that was the thing about that room. We didn't have wires. We didn't have a sound system. We wanted to make sure that there was no way anyone could get in or out of that room. Like I said, it was soundproof. All of those precautions had saved many children over the years. But it also meant that if something went wrong, it might be a while before we knew about it."

"So what happened?"

"Ricky was a sickly child. He often suffered seizures. When your father rescued them, it had been chaos. He had to rush. Luther told him that they needed to go back and get the boy's medicine. But your father didn't have a chance. That wasn't his fault, of course. Normally we would have taken care of it right away. We would have gotten our hands on the medications. That was part of our protocol. We always ask about that when they arrive."

"But not that night," I said.

"No. That night, when the police came, we didn't have time. Ricky had a seizure. A really bad one."

"And he died?" I asked.

"Yes." Dylan Shaykes looked into my eyes. "Can you imagine it? Watching the only person you ever loved die on the floor in front of you. Pounding on the big metal door. Screaming for help."

"And no one could hear," I said.

Dylan nodded. "We sealed up the room after that. No one has been in it since."

We walked some more.

"Luther never forgave, did he?"

"He pretended he did. But that was just to get placed. As soon as he was out, he ran away. I don't know where he's been. He blamed all of us, but your father most of all. He swore that he would get revenge."

"What did he do to my father?"

"I don't know."

"I saw him there. Eight months ago. He was dressed as a paramedic. He took my father away."

He nodded. "I know."

"Bat Lady thinks my father's alive."

"I know."

"Do you?"

Dylan looked at me and I saw the answer before he said it. "No."

I swallowed. "You think . . . ?"

"That Luther killed your father. Yes. I saw him, Mickey. I saw his rage. So, no, I don't think he spared him. I think he took him away and killed him."

"Is that why he burned down the house? For revenge?"

"I assume so."

"And he's still out there."

"Yes."

"So you're still not safe."

"None of us are, Mickey. None of us are safe."

CHAPTER 34

I came home exhausted.

I figured that I would text Ema and start filling her in on my encounter with Dylan Shaykes, but as soon as my head hit the pillow, I started drifting off. It could wait, I thought. In fact, it would probably be better to go over this with her face-to-face.

I fell into a deep sleep.

When I walked to school Monday, I took a slightly different route to avoid the Bat Lady's house. I was not sure why I did that. Or maybe I knew but I didn't want to think about it.

In the past I had thought about all the children who were rescued in that house. Now, for the first time, I started thinking about one specific boy who ended up dying trapped in a room. I hated Luther. I hated what he did to me and my family. One day, I hoped to meet up with him and exact justice.

But part of me now understood. Part of me wondered what it must have been like to be locked in a room, watching the only person you love die—and there is nothing you can do about it.

Bat Lady had explained it to me right at the beginning. The good guys don't always win. We rescue as many as we can. There is an old Arab expression that when one person dies, an entire universe dies. The opposite is true too. If you save a life, even one, you save a universe.

But you can't save them all.

I was about three blocks from the school when I heard the car. It was a red sports car. Troy was driving. He pulled up alongside me and said, "Want a ride?"

"Sure."

I slid low into the passenger seat. The car sat way down. It felt like my butt was practically on the road. Troy shifted into gear and we shot away. "I thought a lot about what we talked about," Troy said. "About Buck."

"Uh-huh," I said. "And?"

"I'm trying to think how to say this." He put his hand through his thick mane of hair, keeping his eyes focused on the road. "Part of the reason I gave you a hard time when you first showed up has to do with your uncle. Myron and my old man don't get along."

"So I gathered. Do you know why?"

Troy shook his head. "It dates back to high school. My dad

was the senior captain on the basketball team when Myron was a sophomore."

Neither one of us had to say *just like us* because we were both thinking it.

"So what happened?"

"I don't know. Do you?"

"No idea," I said.

"Yet they still hate each other all these years later," Troy said.

"Yeah."

"Mickey?"

"What?"

"I don't want that to be our fate," Troy said.

I wanted to say something like *me neither* or *it won't be,* but it all sounded so stupid in my head. I let it pass. I watched Troy driving. He had been looking troubled a lot lately but not like this.

"What aren't you telling me?" I asked.

His jaw clenched as though he was willing himself not to say anything.

"Troy, if you want me to help you . . ."

He turned the wheel sharply to the left and then slowed to a stop. We were still a block away from school. "Buck has been my best friend since we were six—since we had Mr. Ronkowitz in first grade." He stopped the car and turned to me. "Do you have any friends like that, Mickey?"

I felt a deep pang in my chest. "No," I said. "No one."

"You and Ema. You're tight, right?"

"Right."

"Imagine if you'd been that way since you were six. I mean, I'm not saying friends have to know each other a long time. But since we were six. You get what I'm saying?"

"I think so," I said.

Troy closed his eyes and let out a deep breath. "Buck was taking steroids."

For a moment we just sat there, two guys in a car parked on a side street, not saying a word. We let the revelation hang between us. Finally I asked, "When did he start?"

"I don't know. Last spring."

"He just admitted it?"

"Not at first. I asked him about it, though. I could see he was getting bigger. He said I should do them too. I said I didn't need to. Then after you showed up, he started pushing me a little harder. He started saying that I'd always been the leading scorer, but if I didn't get a lot better, you'd take over. Stuff like that. He started getting angrier too. Roid rage, I think they call it, right?"

Roid rage, I knew, was one of the many side effects of steroids. You start losing your temper easily. You grow dark and violent and even suicidal.

Troy shook his head again. "I should have stopped him. I mean, I saw the changes but I didn't do anything, you know? And then . . . then I saw the changes in how Buck was with me."

"What do you mean?"

"My dad once told me that relationships are never fifty-fifty. He said the key was to understand that. Sometimes it's ninety-ten, sometimes ten-ninety. But if you're thinking it's always fifty-fifty, you're going to get yourself in trouble."

"Okay."

"With Buck and me, look, I was the leader, he was the follower. That's just the way it was. I didn't think anything of it. But the last few weeks, it was, like, suddenly that bugged him."

"That you were the leader?"

"Right. I think it was the steroids. Buck started directing his anger toward me too."

I thought about that for a few moments. "Buck wanted you to take steroids too."

"Yes."

"Was he upset when you didn't?"

"Yeah. I mean, he said something like, you think you're too good for them or something. I don't remember his exact words."

"So how was Buck getting the steroids?" I asked.

Troy closed his eyes and said, "Oh man."

"What?"

"I don't want to say."

"Troy, I'm trying to help here."

"It stays between us, right?"

"Where did he get them?"

Troy's eyes opened. He turned toward me and looked me straight in the eye. "His brother."

I think I gasped out loud. "Randy?"

Troy nodded. "He deals out of his father's gym. A lot of people know that."

"But Randy has a huge career ahead of him. Why would he risk that?"

"Are you serious?"

"Yes."

"How do you think he got that huge career? Do you know how many athletes do it—pro, college, and yeah, even high school? It's practically an epidemic. Some get caught, but most of the time they know how to cycle or take some kind of masking agent. Everyone is looking for an edge, Mickey. The other guy is doing it, so they do it. The other guy is going to get that college scholarship, so you do it so you can even the score. After a while, they don't even see it as cheating. They see it as leveling the playing field."

I swallowed. "Is that how you felt, Troy?"

"What?" He put his hand against his chest. "No. Look, I'm telling you the reality. Truth is, I don't need it. I'm a point guard. My game is more finesse. But I get it. Don't you?"

"No," I said. "I wouldn't cheat."

"Really? I've seen how much you love basketball. Suppose everyone else was taking a pill that made them bigger and stronger and you got left behind. You got cut from the team. You weren't any good. And the only reason is, they were taking this pill and you weren't. Are you saying you would *never,* ever take it? That you'd just settle for getting cut and watching others take your spot?"

I shifted in the seat. "That's not the reality."

"But that's how some guys start to see it," Troy said. "You're a special talent. You don't have to worry about that. Or maybe, look, maybe I'm trying to justify what a friend did. I don't know."

I tried to let all of this sink in. According to Troy, Randy Schultz dealt steroids. Was that true? How could I check on that?

Uncle Myron might know.

I thought now to the tense scene I'd witnessed a week ago at Schultz's gym. What was going on between Uncle Myron and Randy? What help did he and his dad want from him that, as a lawyer, Myron couldn't share with me?

"There's something else," Troy said.

I waited.

"I didn't think much of it before all this happened and even after, I mean, whatever I was saying, Buck is still my best friend. I wouldn't believe . . ."

"Wouldn't believe what?"

"Do you know the shed behind the town circle?"

Kasselton had a town circle. On one side of it was the high school. On the other was a bunch of municipal buildings and the YMCA. "No, not really."

"It's behind town hall, near the Y."

"Okay."

"Anyway, a few days before they ran the tests, I was supposed to meet Buck at the circle. We were going to take a couple of laps."

The circle was exactly half a mile in circumference. It was a popular jogging spot.

"I got there early," Troy said, "and I spotted something weird."

"What?"

"I saw Randy and Buck going into that shed."

I was getting confused. "The one behind town hall?"

"Right."

"What kind of shed is this?"

"Well, that's just it. I looked it up. The property is owned by Schultz's gym."

"So it's theirs?"

"I guess. So I followed them to it. When they saw me, they freaked out."

"Freaked out how?"

"They pulled down the shades and came out and acted like it was nothing. But I saw something."

"What?"

Troy took his time. Then at last he said, "Test tubes."

I tried to make that compute. It wouldn't. "Did you ask Buck about them?"

"No."

"Why not?"

"I figured . . . well, I figured that they had something to do with the steroids. You know. Like it was his supply hut or something."

"You don't think that anymore?"

"I don't know. But that was the last time Buck and I talked. Nothing was ever the same. Now he's gone, and I got thrown off the team. So now I'm thinking about what you said. I'm thinking about that shed. And I'm thinking there's some secret in there that could give us all our answers."

CHAPTER 35

Troy and I agreed to meet up that night at the town circle and check out the shed under the cover of darkness. I'd hoped to talk to Ema during lunch because I really needed her take on Luther and my father, not to mention what Troy had told me about Buck and his brother, but Ema had to meet with Mrs. Cannon, her math teacher, during lunch for extra help. She had a big test coming up.

Schoolwork waits for no teenager. Schoolwork doesn't care about your problems.

Around 2:00 P.M., I got a text from Spoon: **Found something huge. When can you get here?**

Ema and Rachel had been copied too. I texted back that I would go right after practice. Ema wrote that she had some homework and would meet me there. Rachel said that she had play tryouts—she was going for the role of Éponine in the school's production of *Les Miz*—so she wouldn't be able to make it, but hoped someone could fill her in later.

Our team.

I thought about the four of us and wanted to shake my head. What chance did we have against guys like Luther? On the one hand, none. On the other hand, we had done pretty darn well so far.

As soon as practice was over, I showered, changed, and hurried to the hospital. The lady behind the desk had gotten to know me by now. She handed me a pass with a minimum of fanfare. I took the elevator up to his floor.

When I walked past the hospital lounge for visiting family members, I spotted Mrs. Spindel, Spoon's mother, sitting in the corner. She stared out the window. Her eyes looked like shattered marbles. I stopped and swallowed. We had not spoken since my first visit after Spoon had been shot. She told me in no uncertain terms that she blamed me:

Oh, I know it's your fault . . .

As though sensing my presence, Mrs. Spindel turned toward where I was standing. For a moment she just looked at me. I wasn't sure what to do. Waving hello seemed foolish. I prepared for another dose of her deserved wrath. But she surprised me this time.

"Thank you, Mickey."

"For what?" I asked.

"For being here. For being his friend."

I shook my head. Her earlier anger had stung, but somehow

this hurt more. I was Spoon's friend? If so, some friend. "How is he?" I asked.

"No change."

I wanted to say something encouraging, but that felt like the exact wrong thing to do. I nodded and waited.

"I'm sorry," she said. "I was being too hard on you. I hope you understand . . ."

"You were right," I said.

"No, Mickey, I wasn't. It wasn't your fault. I can see how much you care about him—and how much he cares about you. That's rare and special. It's just that since you've come to town . . ."

Her words faded away. She didn't have to finish the thought. I got it. I had wanted to move back to the United States. I wanted to make roots in a town like Kasselton. I wanted to be in a real high school and play on a real team, and while I loved my life of travel with my parents, I had craved some normalcy.

So my loving parents had abided my wishes.

Now my father was dead. My mother was a drug addict. And my new friend was lying in a hospital bed, unable to move his legs.

I thought about what Bat Lady said, about how Spoon was meant for great things. I wanted to tell this woman about that, but I knew how stupid it would sound. I didn't get Bat Lady or Elizabeth Sobek or whatever she was called. I always expected my old mentor to be kinder or sweeter or someone

I could relate to. Bat Lady was none of those things. I always felt more puzzled after I left her than before. Sometimes I thought that she had special powers, but then something would happen that would bring me crashing back to reality.

There was no destiny here. No already-determined winner. We could indeed win. And we could indeed die.

Still, Bat Lady had told me Spoon was destined for greatness. She had told me that my father was still alive.

Did she know something?

Did she have some special powers? Or was she just a crazy do-gooder who saved some and lost others?

Mrs. Spindel turned back toward the window, dismissing me, I guess, or giving me permission to visit her son now. I stood there another second and felt a hand on my back. I turned. It was Ema.

"Hey," she said softly.

"Hey."

We started down the corridor and opened the door to Spoon's room. Two doctors walked out with grim expressions. It was another dose of reality.

Spoon looked distracted.

"You okay?" I asked him.

Spoon didn't answer right away.

"Your text said you found something huge?" I said.

"You first," Spoon said.

"What?"

"Tell us about Luther."

So I did. I told them about Dylan Shaykes, about how he'd been rescued as a child, about how my father had rescued Luther, about the death of the little boy Ricky, about how Luther blamed my father. Ema listened in shock. Spoon stayed distracted.

When I finished, before Ema could say a word, Spoon said, "Now tell us about Jared Lowell."

That question puzzled me. "What do you mean?"

"Tell us about your visit to Adiona Island."

"I did already."

Spoon looked up at me. "Tell us again. Everything. Everything that happened from the moment you arrived on that island to the moment you left."

"Why?"

But Spoon just looked at me. He didn't have to say more. So I went through it again—the ferry ride, the walk down the street, the narrow road where Jared lived. I recounted as best as I could the entire conversation Rachel and I had had with Jared Lowell. Spoon interrupted several times, asking for more details, most of which seemed completely irrelevant.

After I was finished, Ema followed up with the first question, but it wasn't for me. It was for Spoon. "What was that all about?"

"You really care about this guy, don't you?" Spoon asked her.

I had never seen him so serious.

"Yes."

"So do you buy it?"

"Buy what?"

"That Jared Lowell was just flirting with you online and decided not to do it anymore for no reason and, oh, decided to go back to Adiona Island?"

Ema looked at me, then back to Spoon. "No, I don't buy it."

"Because his feelings for you were real."

"Well, I could have been fooled—"

"You could be fooled a million different ways, Ema," Spoon said, a hint of impatience in his voice, "but not in this case. Not with the feelings. You could be fooled by the outer trappings. But not by your heart."

We both looked at Spoon, dumbfounded. Who was this guy? As if to show us he was still the same, Spoon arched an eyebrow and said, "I've been reading romance books on the side."

"I still don't see what you're getting at," I said.

"Adiona Island," Spoon said.

"What about it?"

"The name."

I tried not to look as confused as I felt. "What about it?"

"You know who Abeona was, right?"

"What?"

"Abeona, the Roman goddess of outward journeys."

"What does that have to do with—"

"Adiona is her sister," Spoon said.

I froze.

"Adiona is the Roman goddess of safe return. They both

protect children. That's their roles. They are partners. They watch over children—Abeona on their departures, Adiona on their return."

Ema and I stood there, not saying a word.

"Either of you think the name is a coincidence?" Spoon asked.

We didn't answer.

"Neither do I," Spoon said. "You need to go back to that island. You need to go back as soon as you can."

CHAPTER 36

Ema and I started home.

"I'm going this time," Ema said. "I want Jared to look me in the eye and say it was no big thing."

I nodded. "Okay."

"We leave in the morning?"

I nodded again.

"What else?" she asked.

"What do you mean?"

Ema just frowned. "Aren't we past that, Mickey?"

She had a point. "We are," I said.

"So?"

"It's about Troy."

Ema sighed. "Are you still trying to prove he didn't do steroids?"

"Yes."

"And?"

"I think he was set up."

"By?"

"By Buck."

Ema shook her head.

"What?" I said.

"Buck doesn't put ketchup on his French fries without asking Troy first."

"Buck's brother might have been involved."

"How?"

I filled her in on what I'd learned so far. We kept walking. We reached the road where Ema would—before I knew the truth about where she lived and who her mother was—peel off and walk on her own.

"So that's what you're doing now?" Ema asked, when I finished. "You and Troy are going to break into this shed."

"I could use help," I said.

"Me?"

"Sure."

Ema shook her head. "No."

"Why not? This is what we do, Ema. We help people."

"I don't want to help Troy Taylor."

"But this could lead to the truth."

"I don't care, Mickey. You don't get it. He's been cruel to me my whole life."

"Okay, then," I said.

"Okay what?"

"I won't help him either."

"Oh no," Ema said. "You don't get to put that on me."

I stopped. We turned and looked at each other. I was far taller, so she tilted her head up. I knew that it was maybe wrong to think this, but she looked so vulnerable, gazing up at me. Young and innocent, and the idea that those eyes would see something that would hurt her made my heart ache.

Darkness had set in. Her face glowed in the moonlight.

I wanted to protect her. I wanted to protect her always.

"People change, Ema."

She blinked and looked away. "I don't think so, Mickey." Ema took a step back and started toward the woods to the right. "I'm going home," she said. "Don't follow me."

"You're really not going to help me?"

"I'm really not going to help you," she said. "But, Mickey?"

"Yes?"

"If it all goes wrong, I'll still be there for you."

"It won't all go wrong," I said.

But she had already turned away and started down the path.

CHAPTER 37

The town circle was bustling with late-night joggers of all ages, genders, and persuasions. The track was well lit and had no car traffic. It was safe, comfortable, and for those who liked to be seen working out, it offered something of an audience. I stood by a statue of Robert Frost in front of the library on the southern tip of the circle. The municipal buildings and YMCA, not to mention, I guess, the Schultz family shed, were on the other side of Kasselton Avenue.

My phone rang. It was Troy.

"Where are you?" I asked him.

"Look toward the Y."

I did. It was too dark to see much.

"The right side," he said. "Toward the back. I'm holding up my phone."

Now I saw the glow of a phone, a pinprick of light in the dark.

"I see you," I said. "I'm on my way."

I hung up the phone and followed the light. Kasselton Avenue is the town's busiest road. I waited for the light and crossed at the walk. No reason to jaywalk and break any extra laws tonight, thank you very much. I veered toward the YMCA and met up with Troy near the back of the building.

"Thanks for coming," Troy said.

"No problem. Where is this shed?"

"It's down that path. Come on, I'll show you."

We walked on a concrete pathway into the darkness. I glanced behind me. The circle was lit up almost like a distant dome. It provided a modicum of illumination, enough to see the faint outline of a small building maybe thirty yards in front of me.

All the lights were out in the shed.

"Mickey?" Troy whispered.

"Yeah?" I whispered back.

"Buck wouldn't set me up. I don't care what he was taking or doing. He wouldn't do that to me."

"What about Randy?" I asked.

"Maybe," Troy allowed. "But why would he do it?"

"Why would Buck? Why would anyone?"

That question kept coming back to me. Why would anyone want to set Troy Taylor up for a positive drug test? Who gained from it? Who hated him enough . . . ?

Uh-uh, I told myself. No way.

I said that to myself because when I thought about who

hated Troy, the first name that popped into my head was Ema.

I pushed the thought away. This sadly was sometimes how my mind worked. It went places that it shouldn't go.

"I don't know," Troy said.

"So let's see how this plays out."

"Okay," Troy said. "What do we do now?"

I took the lead. We crept down closer to the building. I wasn't sure exactly how to describe the size. When I think of a shed, I think of a place to store tools in the backyard. This was bigger than that, closer to the size of a one-car garage. It was oddly situated too, behind town hall, not far from the police station, the library, and the high school. One would think that this was public land, owned by the town, but for some reason, Buck's father had decided to purchase it.

Why?

I moved toward the shed and tried to look through the darkened windows. I cupped my hand against the glass and leaned in close. Part of me almost expected to see a face jump into view, like a big clown's face with a big smile, and then I'd startle back, screaming.

Stop it, I scolded myself.

There was nothing to see. It was too dark.

Troy was trying to peer into the window too. "Make out anything?" he whispered to me.

"No."

We circled the building. I could see why you might call it

a shed. It was flimsier than a real building, made out of some kind of prefab material you'd find in the lot of a hardware store. There were two more windows in the back, but the shades were drawn.

"So now what?"

I spotted a back door. Good. From this angle, no one near the circle could see anything. Come to think of it, even in the front, which more or less faced the circle, no one could really see anything.

"We check the door," I said.

Sometimes you get lucky. Sometimes you put a hand on a doorknob and turn it and the door is unlocked. That wasn't what happened here. Locked. I checked the area around the knob. The lock looked pretty cheap.

Not long ago, Ema and I had tried to break into Bat Lady's house. I had taken a credit card from my wallet and tried to open it via the way I had seen a thousand times on television. It hadn't worked. That lock had been old and so it simply gave way. But after that I got curious, so I started searching the Internet to learn how to pick locks. In truth, it isn't easy. If there was a deadbolt, it was impossible, but if this was a standard spring bolt, I could maybe get away with it.

It was a spring bolt.

Bingo.

I took out my credit card and started to work it. You don't really pick a lock with a credit card. You jimmy it open. I stuck the card in the crack between the door and the frame and slid it down to the lock. I bent the card toward the knob, hoping to slide the corner underneath. Nothing much happened. I put my shoulder against the door. The key is, open it fast when you feel the pop. That's what the websites said.

It wasn't working.

I pushed a little harder with my shoulder. The cheap material gave way. I could feel something bend. I looked back at Troy. He shrugged and said, "I can do it if you want."

I shook my head. I was already there. My fingers might not be nimble, but there was nothing like a strong shoulder. I rocked back, hit the door a little harder with my shoulder, and the door flew open.

Breaking and entering. Again.

I was already cooking up various excuses, just in case we got caught. Example: We had heard someone calling for help maybe. Or we just tried the door and it was already open, so we just came to check and make sure everything was okay.

Right. Like either one of those would fly.

But at least I had a Get-Out-of-Jail-Free card with me: the police chief's son. I slowly stepped into the shed. Troy followed me inside. There was a wall right in front of us dividing the space into two rooms. The lights were out, so we couldn't see much more.

"You take the room on the left," I said to him. "I'll take the room on the right."

"Should we use our flashlights?"

"Let's keep the beams low, beneath the window height."

"Okay," Troy said. "Mickey?"

"What?"

"What are we looking for?"

"A big sign with the word *clue* on it."

Troy laughed at that. "I'm serious."

"A laptop, for one thing. Files maybe. But in truth, I'm not sure. I think it's one of those 'we'll know it when we see it' kinda things."

"Got ya."

We split up then. I did as I suggested and kept my smartphone's flashlight beam pointed at the floor. I could make out what looked like a table in the center of the room. I moved toward it. I risked lifting the beam a little higher to see what was on the table.

It looked like chemistry class.

Test tubes, beakers, flasks, and the like littered the table. I started to wonder if there was a Bunsen burner here too. I turned off the flashlight and tried to think for a moment.

A lab.

Why?

I thought about what Troy had told me—about Randy dealing drugs. Could this be, I don't know, a drug lab of some kind? How do you make steroids? I had no idea. Could that be what this was?

Again: no idea.

The room was sparkling clean. I saw a metal cylinder on the right. Stainless steel cabinets lined the wall. I put my hand on one. It felt cold to the touch. I took hold of the handle and pulled the cabinet open. It opened like a refrigerator. I felt cold air. I lifted the flashlight so that I could see inside.

There might as well have been a sign saying CLUE.

"Ew, gross," I whispered to myself.

Troy stuck his head around the wall. He shined the flashlight up in my face before aiming it toward the open cabinet. "Wait, is that . . . ?"

"I think so, yeah," I said.

The cabinet was loaded up with small plastic containers that I recognized from our drug testing. There was a yellow liquid inside. In short, the cabinet was loaded up with . . .

"Urine samples," I said.

"Nasty."

I made a face and gently lifted one of the specimen cups.

Suddenly I heard Troy's panicked voice. "What was that?"

I turned toward him. "What?"

He leapt toward the window, nearly knocking the urine specimen from my hand. I followed him. We ducked down low and peeked outside. At first, I didn't see anything, just the streetlights in the distance.

"What?" I asked.

"Might have been my imagination, but I-I thought I saw . . ."

And then they became clearer. Flashlights. Flashlights that were heading toward us. Not small flashlights like on our smartphones, but big, thick ones, the kind used by . . .

"It's my dad!" Troy yell-whispered. "We gotta get out of here!"

He didn't have to tell me twice. We ran for the door, bumping into the table. Beakers crashed to the floor. I heard a voice yell out. An adult voice.

Like the voice of a cop.

Troy got to the door first, but I was right behind him. We ran straight back, trying to keep the building between those flashlights and our bodies. Troy jumped behind a big boulder. I joined him. Up the hill on Kasselton Avenue, I could now see the whirling light atop a parked police car.

"Oh man," I said.

"Split up," Troy said. "You head into the woods, I'll go behind the Y and try to circle to the street. If I can get there, I can divert them."

That made sense. I turned and ran into the woods behind me. This sounded easier than it actually was. It was dark now. There was only the faintest light coming from the distant streetlights. Woods have a lot of, well, trees. So put it altogether: running in a dark place with a lot of trees.

Not easy.

The third time I kissed bark, it dawned on me that I'd have to slow down. What choice did I have? If I kept running face-first into trees, I would probably knock myself unconscious. I started moving like Frankenstein, keeping my hands out in front of me, feeling my way.

"Stop! Police!"

The voice made me duck behind a tree. I risked a look. Two of the cops—or least, two flashlights—were entering the woods now. Because they had flashlights, they didn't really need to worry too much about smashing into trees. They could move at a pretty fast clip.

Oh man, I was in trouble.

Those dumb excuses—I heard someone call for help, the door lock was broken before we got there—started flooding back in, but I knew that they would just help sink me. Bat Lady would not be able to get me out of this one, and I somehow doubted that Buck's father would say that I had permission to break the lock on his shed door and shatter a bunch of beakers.

Yep, I was in trouble.

I stayed behind the tree but I could tell from the bouncing flashlights that they were getting closer.

Think, Mickey.

The fact was, the two officers had one advantage over me: They could see. I had one advantage over them, albeit temporarily: I could hide. But the hiding could only last a little longer. The flashlights would discover me. But then again, if I put my flashlight on too, yes, they'd see me, but it would also even the playing field.

There was one other thing to consider—the police officers might be armed—but this was Kasselton, not Newark. In towns like this, officers don't pull their guns, especially on suspects running through the woods.

I flipped on the flashlight and ran.

"Stop! Police!"

I didn't know which was worse: breaking into that shed or running away from the police. Either way, I picked up my pace. They were fast. I was faster. More than that, I did figure out an advantage. I would shine my flashlight in front of me, plan out the path, turn off the flashlight, confuse them with that, turn it on again when I needed it.

Then I got a break.

The woods started to grow less dense. The officers behind me were in the thick of it now. I was nearly out. Once I barreled through, I came into a clearing behind the Kasselton Mall.

Perfect.

There were still plenty of cars in the lot. That was a bonus too. I hurried over to Target because it was the largest store in the mall. I found a corner kiosk in the appliance department where I could see both entrances. If the police entered one, I could hurry out the other or even hide in the vast space of the store.

But the cops didn't come inside.

At the end of the day, I was just a kid who maybe broke into a big tool shed. It might be interesting, but it wasn't as though a SWAT team was going to be called out.

Half an hour after entering the Target, I went through the mall and exited out the Sears on the other side. There were no police. I started down Hobart Gap Road toward Uncle Myron's house.

So what do I do now?

Should I text Troy? That seemed iffy. If he'd been caught and I texted him, the police might see that we were communicating. I should wait and let him contact me. But then again, would he? Wouldn't he logically think the same thing about contacting me and also wait?

I wasn't sure it mattered.

I tried to put together what I had learned in Mr. Schultz's shed. Start from the beginning: One, Troy had seen Buck and his brother, Randy, both of whom he claimed used steroids, go into that shed with test tubes. Now that I'd been inside the shed, it was clearly some kind of laboratory. It could have something to do with making the PEDs—performance-enhancing drugs. Maybe Randy or Buck was tinkering with, I don't know, their formula.

I frowned. I'm not sure Buck could spell the word *chemistry*, nonetheless start fiddling with complex compounds.

Then I remembered the urine samples.

I don't know how many were stored in that cabinet—and, ew, I hoped none fell on the floor as we ran out—but what could Buck and Randy be doing with them?

Hmm.

I had read somewhere that steroid cheaters would often use someone else's urine to beat the system. Here was how it worked: You hid a urine sample on you when you went to the test. When you entered the bathroom stall to urinate, you switched your sample with one you knew was clean.

Could that be it?

Possible, except for one thing. There were probably a hundred urine samples in storage. We only get tested once or maybe twice a year. Why so many?

I was missing something.

I didn't know what. In a sense, it didn't matter. Tomorrow I would head back to Adiona Island. There was some kind of clue there, some kind of link between that island and the Bat Lady and the Abeona Shelter and maybe even Luther and my father. I wanted to help here. I wanted to figure out why Troy had been set up and by whom. But it wasn't my priority.

Except . . .

I had an idea. I took out my phone and called Brandon Foley. He answered on the third ring. "What's up?" he said.

"I'm about two blocks from your house. You free?"

"Sure," Brandon said. "Anything to avoid studying for this physics test."

As I got closer, I heard the comforting sound of a dribbling basketball. Brandon was in his driveway again, working on his game. He tossed me the ball when he saw me coming. I stopped and took a jumper. *Swish*. He threw the ball back to me—"courtesy" is a universal basketball concept—but I just held the ball.

"You have your phone?" I asked.

"It's in the house. Why?"

"I may need you to text Troy."

"Why can't you?"

"Because he and I . . ."

"What?"

And that was when I stopped. I liked Brandon. I really did. But I wasn't sure that I wanted to confess to him that I had just done something illegal. He was president of the student council and all those other things. He took his responsibilities as basketball captain seriously.

Could he be trusted?

Sure, Brandon had been the one to get me involved in helping Troy, but what would he say if I told him that I'd just broken into a storage shed and run away from the cops?

Would he tell?

I had thought that I could ask Brandon to contact Troy for me, so that it wouldn't get traced back to my phone. But now I wondered whether that was a good move.

"You and he what?" Brandon asked again.

"Nothing."

"So why did you want to see me?"

In a way, Brandon couldn't help me with this. I would hear from Troy or I wouldn't. It didn't change anything. Brandon couldn't help with the break-in. He couldn't help answer why I had found urine samples in that shed or really anything that could cast light on this situation.

So even if I did trust him, even if I believed that he only had my and Troy's best interests at heart, what was the point of telling him?

Answer: nothing. There was no point.

But there was still one key to all this—one person who could answer all my questions about that shed, about illegal steroids, about why Troy had tested positive. It kept circling back to that same question:

Why had Buck left the town of Kasselton?

There was only one person who, it seemed, could really answer that question for me.

Buck himself.

"Where's Buck?" I asked.

Brandon looked puzzled by the question. "I told you. He lives with his mom."

"Where does she live?"

"I don't remember," Brandon said. "Somewhere in Maine or Massachusetts."

"You have no idea?"

"I remember he used to go there a lot in the summer." And then Brandon added something that changed everything: "He'd go boating or fishing off the island."

I stood there. I was gripping the basketball so hard, I thought it might pop.

"Island?" I said.

"Yeah, his mom lives on an island. It's got a weird name. Like Apollonia or Adonis or something with an *A*."

I swallowed. "Adiona?"

"Yeah, that's it," Brandon said. "Buck's mom lives on Adiona Island."

CHAPTER 38

Ema and I barely talked on the way back up to Adiona Island.

The seas were choppy this morning. We stood at the front of the ferry. The wind ripped at our faces. I watched Ema's pale complexion redden under the onslaught. She didn't care. I didn't care either.

We had stopped trying to piece this together. There comes a time when you need to put all the theories aside. Mrs. Friedman had a poster in her classroom with a saying from Sherlock Holmes. I don't remember the exact quote, so I'm paraphrasing, but it says that it's a mistake to theorize before you have all the facts because then you twist facts to suit theories instead of the other way around.

We simply had no theories anymore.

We needed more facts.

The wind picked up. Everyone else had ducked inside to escape. Ema and I did not. We stared out as the island emerged from the fog.

"Mickey?"

The wind snatched away the word, making it hard to hear her.

"What?" I shouted back.

"I'm scared."

"We'll be fine," I said.

"I love when you're condescending."

"I'm trying to be comforting."

"Same thing, Mickey." Ema looked up at me. "It's cute that you want to be the hero, but I'd rather you were just honest, okay?"

I put my arm around her. It was just to keep her warm. Nothing else. She moved in closer and rested her head against my chest. We stood like that as the ferry moved closer to the port. I could almost feel something change as we docked. There was something in the air on this island.

A tension. An electricity.

We both felt it.

I moved my arm away. I still hadn't heard from Troy, but then again, I hadn't contacted him either. Spoon had tried to find where on the island Buck's mother lived, but he couldn't come up with anything. It didn't matter. The island was small.

We would find the house.

Meanwhile, there was still the other matter. Ema had to go face-to-face with Jared Lowell, this online persona who had, it seemed, captured her heart. We started down the same road I had walked with Rachel. The wind grew less powerful as we moved inland, but it never left.

"Do you remember what Bat Lady said to me?" Ema asked.

"She said a lot of things."

"At the very end. Right before she got in that car and she drove off with that shaved head guy."

I did remember. "She asked if you loved the boy."

"She didn't ask. She said it. Like she knew."

I nodded. "Right."

"Do you remember what she said after that?"

That line I remembered verbatim: "'It will hurt.'"

"Right."

"And then you asked what will. And she said the truth."

We were nearing Jared's road now. If the island had seemed quiet last time, it seemed completely abandoned now. We had not seen anyone or even a passing car since leaving the dock.

"I think," Ema said, "we may be coming close to that truth."

We made the turn onto Jared Lowell's road. It was completely still, silent. I almost expected one of those ghost-town tumbleweeds to blow across the street. Ema turned to me and said, "Which door?"

I pointed up the block a bit. "That one."

"Okay, good."

"Do you want me to wait here?"

Ema thought about it. "No, come with me."

"You sure?"

"Yeah," she said. "If this is going to hurt, I want you to be there for me."

We started up that same cracked-concrete path. I knocked. Ema and I stood there, adjusting our shoulders and then our heads and doing that dumb stuff you do when you're waiting for a door to open.

Eventually we heard footsteps heading toward us. I glanced at Ema. She gave me a hesitant smile. The door opened.

But it wasn't Jared. It was his mother.

She frowned at me. "You were here a few days ago."

"Yes, ma'am," I said.

"What do you want?"

She said it as though it were an accusation.

"We're here to see Jared."

"What do you want with him?"

I didn't know how to answer that. I looked toward Ema. She said, "We're his friends."

"From the Farnsworth School?"

"No, ma'am," I said.

"Then where are you from?"

"Kasselton, New Jersey," Ema replied.

A look of horror crossed the woman's face. She leaned

toward us, baring her teeth like a feral dog. Her eyes were wide. "Get out of here!" she screamed. "Get off this island and never come back!"

She slammed the door so hard that we nearly fell off the stoop.

Ema and I stood there, trying unsuccessfully not to look flabbergasted.

After some time had passed, Ema said, "What the heck was that?"

"I have no idea."

"Did you see how she reacted when she heard where we're from?"

I nodded.

"What could that have to do with my online relationship with her son?"

"Same answer," I said.

"You have no idea?"

"Bingo."

"So now what? Do we start searching for Buck?"

I thought about it. "Did you notice that tennis club on the way in?"

"The snooty-looking one?"

"Right. When Rachel and I were here last time, Jared said something about having to get to his job at the club. I mean, there may be more than one club on this island—"

"No, it's that one," Ema said. "Look at this street. This is where the workers live. I bet ninety percent of the people who live here work at that tennis club. The bigger problem is, look at us. You're wearing jeans. I'm wearing, well, not tennis whites."

"I have an idea," I said.

We started back down the street toward the main road. We turned right. The tennis club was up ahead. I thought that maybe there would be a guard or a gate, but this was the kind of island where you didn't need that. Guards at clubs were there to keep out the riffraff. This island had no riffraff. Just members and staff.

We started down the entrance road when a young man in tennis whites with a sweater tied around his neck hurried toward us. "May I help you?"

"No," I said. "We're fine."

We kept walking toward the clubhouse. I thought that maybe Mr. Tied Sweater would let us be. He didn't. He ran alongside us and said, "Uh, excuse me?"

"Yes?"

"Why are you here?"

I had expected this. I had hoped, though, to get lucky and walk around a little more and maybe spot our boy, but that was not to be. Still, we kept walking and looking as we spoke. "My name is Will. This is my sister, Grace."

Ema nodded. We kept walking and scanning for Jared.

"Yeah, okay. What can I do for you? This club has a strict dress code. Neither one of you is adhering to it."

"We are here seeking employment," I said.

Tied Sweater was getting annoyed that we wouldn't stop walking. "I don't think we are hiring at the current time."

"Oh, that's too bad," Ema said.

We were at the door to the clubhouse. I pushed through. "Maybe we could fill out an application. Just to keep it on file. In case someone quits."

"We require references. Do you have them?"

"Yes, we do." It was time to take a chance. "Jared Lowell will recommend us."

"Oh," Tied Sweater said, suddenly smiling. His whole persona changed. Jared clearly had some clout. "You're both friends of Jared's?"

"Close friends," said Ema.

"Well, that changes things," he said.

"He's working today, right?"

"What? No. In fact, I figured that's why you're here."

I said, "Huh?"

"Jared just left for the ferry. He should be taking off in, oh"—he looked at his watch—"fifteen minutes. The applications are in the back. If you'd like to sit in the—"

But Ema and I were already back outside and sprinting toward the ferry. I was surprised at how Ema was able to keep up with me, but then again, determination counts for a lot.

Still, there wasn't much time. I did a quick calculation and realized that we wouldn't arrive before Jared boarded the next ferry.

Now what?

Then the answer came to me: I could break more laws.

"This way," I said.

"What?"

The summer population here was under two thousand people. That meant there wasn't much crime or need for law enforcement. People didn't lock up their homes.

Or their bikes.

We found two in a driveway on the right. Ema and I hopped on and started peddling. Three minutes later, we spotted Jared sitting on a bench by the dock. When he saw us coming, Jared Lowell shielded his eyes from the sun with his hand and said, "You again."

"Yep. And look who I brought."

I turned and looked at Ema. I couldn't help it. Part of me thought that this was probably not how Ema wanted to look the first time she saw her "great love" in person—sweaty, out of breath, disheveled—and a really small pathetic part of me took some small pleasure in that.

Ema looked at him. He looked at her. I took a step back.

"Hey," Ema said to him.

"Hey," Jared said back.

Ema seemed to be studying him. He started to shift under her gaze.

"I'm sorry," Jared Lowell said.

Ema did not reply. She tilted her head, looking at him as though he were some kind of odd experiment.

"I should have told you," he said.

273

"Told me what?"

"Excuse me?"

"What were you going to tell me, Jared?"

His feet shifted again. The ferry had arrived. The passengers began to disembark. "You know. I mean, I should have told you that I didn't want to e-mail you anymore."

I expected her to be hurt or crushed, but it was as though seeing him in person had given her an odd strength. "Why didn't you?"

"Why didn't I tell you?"

"Yeah," Ema said, "start with that."

"I don't know." Jared gave a big shrug. "It was wrong. Your friend here and I talked about it. I was going to get in touch."

"So you wanted to, what, break up with me?"

He looked so uncomfortable, even I felt bad for him. "Well, yeah."

"Why?"

"What do you mean, why?"

"What's your favorite color?"

"What?"

"Just tell me, Jared. What's your favorite color?"

Jared opened his mouth, but no words came out. Ema looked at me and shook her head.

"What?" I said.

"It's not him."

"What do you mean it's not him?"

"Give me some credit, Mickey. I thought that as soon as I saw him in person, but after talking to him for just these few seconds . . ." Ema turned back to him. "You're not the guy who talked to me online, are you?"

"What? Sure I am. Jared Lowell. You saw my Facebook page."

Ema shook her head. "Yes, Jared, it was your Facebook page. And, yes, you clearly knew about it. But it wasn't you, was it?"

"What are you talking about?" He tried to laugh it off, but it wasn't happening. "Of course it's me. Look, we had something. It was great, I guess, but it was just online. It wasn't real."

"Quick: What's your favorite color?"

"Uh, blue."

"What's your favorite food?"

"Pizza."

"What's your favorite place?"

"The hidden cove on the west side of this island."

The color drained from Ema's face. "Oh no . . ."

"What?" I said.

She turned to me. "He got that last one right."

"So?" I was confused. "Maybe you were wrong. Maybe he was the one—"

"He got the color wrong. He got the food wrong. Don't you see?"

Jared started to walk past us. "Look, I got a ferry to catch."

I put my hand against his chest. "You're not going anywhere."

Jared Lowell looked down at my hand. "You serious?"

"Don't move, Jared."

"Who do you think—?"

"Don't. Move."

He heard the tone, raised his hands, and stayed where he was. Ema folded at the waist as though someone had punched her in the stomach. I hurried toward her. "Ema?"

"Don't you get it?"

"Get what?"

"His favorite place. It was someplace on this island."

"So?"

"So if it wasn't him, who else do we know who would know this island?"

Now I was the one who looked horror stricken. "No," I said.

She nodded.

"It can't be," I said.

"But it has to be," Ema said. "It was Buck. Buck was the one I met online."

CHAPTER 39

Jared sat between Ema and me. His head was lowered in his hands.

"It started out as a prank," he said. "I didn't like the idea. I didn't want to be part of it at all."

He kept his head in his hands. Ema kept looking off, lost in thought, trying to put all the pieces together. She had been so sure that the feelings were real, and yet now she knew that it was a ruse by her longtime nemesis. It wasn't computing for her.

"So you know Buck," I said.

"Yes."

"How?"

"He's my cousin. Our moms are sisters. They both grew up on this island. When Aunt Ina met Uncle Boris, she moved to Kasselton. My family stayed here. Buck and I spent every summer together on this island. After the divorce, Aunt Ina moved back here."

I couldn't tell whether Ema was listening or not.

"So what happened?" I asked.

"Buck knew that I almost never used my Facebook. I don't like social media. So one day he asked me if he could use it to get revenge on someone. I didn't like it, but he said some girl had made up a nickname for him, started to call him Mr. Pee Pee Pants."

"Wee Wee Pants," I corrected.

Ema shot me a look. I just shrugged back at her. The charge wasn't really true. Buck had been picking on us, and Ema had countered with some line about Buck being called Mr. Wee Wee Pants. It had been nothing, really.

"Whatever. Buck said the nickname was sticking. Other kids were calling him that now. He said my profile would be perfect to use because Ema already had a crush on a tall basketball player."

We sat there for a moment saying nothing. All three of us knew who Buck meant. No one bothered spelling out the obvious.

"See, Buck found out your mom was someone famous and so he went to that board and started communicating with you. I don't know what he really hoped would happen. That you'd say embarrassing things or maybe he'd just make you fall in love with him and then cruelly dump you. I really don't know what he intended."

"But you just said it," Ema said.

"Huh?"

A tear formed in her eye. "He made me fall for him and then he cruelly dumped me."

Jared closed his eyes and let loose a long breath. "No, Ema, that's not what happened." He stood and started pacing. He rubbed his chin. "I don't know how much more to say."

"She's owed the truth," I said.

A sad smile came to Jared's face. "If only it was that simple."

"Just tell us."

He stopped pacing. "It worked the other way around, I guess."

"What do you mean?" Ema said.

"Buck fell for you."

Ema looked at me. I had nothing to add to that.

"He fell and he fell hard. You have to understand. You really didn't know Buck. I know, I know, but . . . It's confusing. Buck loved it up here. On this island, he could be himself. He was relaxed and happy and really the kindest, sweetest guy."

I tried to picture it, but the picture wouldn't hold. "That's not the guy we know."

"That's my point. Your town. Kasselton, right? Your town with all the popular kids and the sports and the pressure to succeed and get into the right colleges . . . it warped Buck. He couldn't handle it. He always had to be something he wasn't just to fit in."

I thought about that. I thought about the pressure in that

town, the type-A pushy parents, the yelling on the sidelines, the grade grubbing—and then add in for Buck the pressure of the successful brother and maybe losing his starting job.

Jared moved closer to Ema. "But with you," he said, "Buck felt like he found himself. You were so real. You didn't care what the other kids thought of you. He so envied that. When he was online with you, once he got over his own stupidity, he started to open up. He could be himself, pretending to be, well, me."

There were tears in Ema's eyes now. There were tears in Jared's too.

"So what happened?" I asked.

"Buck was a mess. He felt trapped, like he was being pulled in all these different directions. He was scared."

"Of what?" Ema asked.

"Of everything. He wanted to tell you the truth, Ema. But he didn't know how you'd react. He didn't know if you'd hate him once you knew that he'd been lying to you this whole time or if you'd forgive him for the past. He thought you'd reject him once you knew."

I flashed back to my recent conversation with Ema about Troy. I had told her that people change. She was the one who didn't seem to believe it.

"But like I said," Jared continued, "he felt trapped. It may sound like nothing now, but what would his friends say? Wouldn't they all dump on him if he told them he'd fallen in love with you? I know that sounds silly, but these guys had been his whole life. He couldn't just turn his back on that either."

"So," Ema said, "he chickened out."

Jared said nothing.

"That's it, right?"

"The ferry is about to leave," Jared said. "I have to go."

"Where's Buck?" I asked.

"Does it matter?" Jared turned to Ema. "He doesn't want to see you. Isn't that enough? It's over."

The ferry whistle blew last call.

I stood up to block his way, but Ema shook her head. She was right. He had said his piece. I let him pass.

"You should both come with me," Jared said.

"Why?" I asked.

"You need to leave this island."

Ema shook her head. "No."

"Please," Jared said. "There's nothing left here for you but more heartache."

"That's okay." Ema stood up. "I'll just have to deal with more heartache."

CHAPTER 40

Jared made it to the ferry just before it pulled out.

Ema and I stood side by side. "We need to find Buck," she said.

"Okay. How?"

"The aunt."

"Jared's mother?"

"Yes."

I frowned. "She seemed like a font of information."

But Ema had already started walking away. "Come on," she said. "We need to return the bikes before someone notices they're missing."

We pedaled back to the driveway where we had "borrowed" the bicycles. There was no movement. We put the bikes back where they'd been and started up the road toward Jared Lowell's house.

"Buck," I said.

"I know."

"What are you thinking?" I asked her.

"What do you mean?"

"About it being Buck. About Buck falling for you."

She kept her eyes on the road. "On the one hand, I know that online is not real life. But on the other hand, maybe there is something more real about being online."

"How so?"

"Online, it's kind of like you're in a vacuum without outside pressures. Buck didn't have to worry about being in his brother's shadow. He didn't have to worry if Troy or his friends would mock him because he liked me."

"So what you're saying is, maybe you saw the real Buck?"

"Maybe."

"And?"

"And I fell hard for him."

I shook my head. "For Buck?"

"Weren't you the one who told me people change?"

"And weren't you the one who told me that they didn't?"

"Good point."

Ema increased her speed, moving ahead of me and ending the conversation. We were about fifty yards from Jared's street when Ema ducked behind a tree. She signaled for me to do the same. She was behind the only tree close by, so I joined her.

"What's going on?" I whispered.

She gestured toward the road. "See that woman with the shopping bag?"

I took a quick peek. There indeed was a woman carrying a brown grocery bag. "What about her?"

"That's Buck's mom. I saw her a few times at school concerts and stuff."

Buck's mom turned and disappeared down Jared Lowell's street. When she was out of sight, Ema hurried out from behind the tree. I stayed with her. We slowed when we reached the turn.

"She doesn't know me," I said. "I can keep following her."

But there was no need. Buck's mother broke to the left, took out her key, and opened the door to what I assumed was her house.

Right next door to Jared's.

"The sisters live next to each other," I said.

Ema nodded. "Makes sense."

"So now what?"

Ema started biting one of her black-polished fingernails. This island was starting to give me the creeps. Maybe in part it was the name, Adiona (duh, you think?), and all this talk about heartache and hurt, but for a second, I wanted us to listen to Jared Lowell and just get off this crazy island now. I didn't know where Buck was or what he was doing. I didn't care. I wanted to go home. I wanted to go home not just for me but, even more so, for Ema.

Jared had told us that she'd find heartache on this island. Bat Lady had warned us that the answer would hurt her. I didn't want anyone or anything to hurt Ema anymore. I didn't want anything to hurt Rachel or Spoon either, but the truth was, since I had entered their lives, they had all taken devastating hits. Rachel had been shot and lost her mother. Spoon had been shot and now lay paralyzed in a hospital bed.

If something happened to Ema . . .

"I'm going to knock on the door," Ema said.

"I'll go with you."

"No."

"What?"

She turned and looked up at me. "Not this time, Mickey. Okay? Just trust me on this."

I didn't know what to say, so I just stood there. Ema walked to the door. She raised her fist, hesitated for a moment, and then knocked on the door. Time stood still. After what seemed like an eternity, the door opened. When Buck's mother saw who it was, her hand flew to her mouth as she choked back a cry.

Ema stepped forward. "My name is—"

"You're Ema," Buck's mother finished for her.

Ema looked confused. "Yes. But how did you—"

Buck's mother opened the door. "Please, come inside."

CHAPTER 41

Time didn't stand still. It just passed by really, really slowly.

For the first ten minutes, I sat on the curb in front of the house. I got antsy. I stood and started walking just a little up the street, then a little down the street, hoping to catch a glimpse of something—*anything*—in the windows.

But there was nothing.

Another ten minutes passed. Then another. People walked by me. They eyed me with suspicion. It was clear to them I didn't belong here. This was a very small road on a very small island. Visitors didn't often loiter.

Ten more minutes passed.

What the heck was going on in there?

I stopped looking at the time and started looking at the sky. The sun shone down on my face. I closed my eyes and soaked it in. I stopped thinking about Ema and Buck. I stopped thinking about Troy's drug test. I even stopped thinking about my own Butcher of Lodz, the sandy-haired man named Luther.

I thought about my mom and dad.

You often hear that you only get one life and that life isn't a dress rehearsal. That was true, but it felt more direct to me. Simply put, this was it. What you're doing right now is life. This moment, every moment impacts and builds on the next. I could think about the days when my father was alive and my mother was sober. I could dream about going back in time to that moment and altering it, but that would never happen.

Time only goes forward.

My cell phone rang. I looked down and saw that it was Uncle Myron. I was about to hit ignore but I decided to answer it.

"Hey, Myron. I need to ask you something."

"Where are you?"

"It's not important," I said. "Why did Randy Schultz want your help?"

"I already told you. I can't talk about it."

"Did it have something to do with steroids?"

Silence.

"Because I know Buck took steroids. And I know Randy dealt them. Did he get caught? Is that why he needed your help? Is that why you turned him down?"

"Mickey?"

"Yes."

"Where are you?"

"I'm right, aren't I?"

"I told you. I can't talk about it. Attorney-client privilege. Where are you, Mickey?"

The door to Buck's house finally swung open.

"I'll talk to you tonight," I said, and hit end before Myron could say anything more.

Have you ever seen one of those horror movies where someone goes into a house one way and then they come out another, like maybe they're a zombie now or their hair is gray or they're possessed? Like they walked through some portal and completely transformed into something else?

That was what I thought about as I looked at Ema.

She was still dressed the same. The black was still black. The tattoos were still the same. The silver jewelry gleamed just as it had gleamed before. But somehow everything about her seemed different. I know how crazy that sounds. Uncle Myron had told me that when my dad was about my age, he went inside Bat Lady's house and came out a different person. It almost felt like that, as if Ema had gone through the closet to Narnia and come back again. There was a knowing in her eyes, a maturity in her face.

She looked somehow more grown-up.

Or maybe, after all I had seen on this crazy island, I was big-time projecting.

She didn't so much walk toward me as float. She kept her head up high. Her eyes didn't meet mine like they always did. Instead she looked past me and just kept walking.

"Ema?"

"Let's go," she said, and even her voice sounded more mature. "We can still catch the next ferry."

"Wait, what happened in there?"

She didn't reply. She just kept walking.

"Ema?"

"It's over," she said.

"What's over?"

"Come on. I want to be on that ferry."

"What do you mean, 'it's over'?"

She kept moving faster and faster as though she needed to put distance between herself and that house.

"Did you talk to Buck?"

She didn't stop. I put a hand on her arm. She shrugged it off. I jumped in front of her, blocking her path. I tried to make my voice as gentle as I could.

"What happened in there?"

"I can't tell you," she said.

"What do you mean, you can't tell me?"

"I promised."

She pushed past me and headed down the road. I caught up to her.

"You're kidding, right?"

"No."

"This has to be a joke," I said, which was dumb because I knew that she wasn't kidding and that this was the furthest thing from a joke.

"Remember when you couldn't tell me about who shot Rachel and her mother?"

"You're still mad about that? I told you. It wasn't my secret to tell."

She held up a hand. "You have it wrong."

"Oh?"

"I'm not mad about it at all. I understand now. I'm using your example so you'll understand. I can't tell you. I made a promise."

I frowned. "To Buck?"

"It doesn't matter, Mickey. I can't tell you."

I jumped in front of her again. "This isn't the same thing. Buck isn't Rachel. I came all this way with you. I'm a part of it. I want to know."

Ema shook her head. "Sometimes you're better off not knowing."

"Really? You're going to pull that line on me?"

She walked away from me.

My hands formed fists and I shouted, "I didn't come here just for you."

"I know."

"I came to find Buck for myself."

She nodded without slowing her pace. "To help Troy."

"To find the truth."

"You'll find it soon enough," she said.

"What does that mean?"

But Ema didn't speak again. Not on the road. Not on the ferry or the bus. Not even a good-bye when we went our separate ways back in Kasselton.

CHAPTER 42

Spoon said, "Let it go."

Rachel and I were back in his room. I was filling them in on what had happened on Adiona Island.

"How can I let it go?"

"Ema is, like, totally awesome, right?"

"Right."

"And you trust her one hundred percent, right?"

"Right."

"So why stop trusting her now?" Spoon asked. "She said it's best if you don't know. So guess what? It's best that you don't know."

I looked at Rachel. She shrugged. I looked back at Spoon. He pushed his glasses up his nose and met my eye. Bat Lady had said that he was meant for great things. I started thinking back to the beginning of this, that first day when he introduced himself to me by asking if I wanted to use his spoon. It had been his idea how to get into that computer in the school office, his idea to get into Ashley's locker, his idea even how to get into school the night he was shot. It was Spoon who had told us to go to the Farnsworth School and to Adiona Island twice.

I had always thought that I was the leader of this group.

But maybe it was Spoon.

As though reading my mind, Spoon gave a small nod and said, "Give her time."

"So now what?" Rachel asked.

"Nothing," Spoon said. "Ema said it's over. It's over."

I shook my head. "I don't buy it."

"Neither do I," Spoon said. "But we can't force it. You want the egg to hatch on its own. You don't want to break it open. Do you see?"

Everyone in my life was talking like a fortune cookie all of a sudden.

"You break it open if you're hungry," I said.

"Stop playing with my metaphors. You got basketball practice, right? Go."

He was right.

"And," Rachel said, "I heard about your good news, so it should be a fun time."

I turned to her. "What good news?"

"You didn't hear?"

"No, what?"

"They overturned Troy's positive drug test. He's back on the team."

CHAPTER 43

I didn't know what to make of that. I hurried over to practice and started to dress. Troy wasn't there, but the mood was definitely buoyant. Guys slapped each other five. A few came over to me and slapped me five too. They thanked me. They gave me fist bumps.

I tried to think about what I might have done.

When I got out to the gym, I spotted Troy shooting under his familiar center basket. A bunch of guys surrounded him and threw him passes. Troy was a point guard, the shortest starter on the team, but he had deadly aim from three-point land. He knocked down four shots in a row. The guys all clapped and cheered.

When I started toward him, Troy broke into a smile. "Mickey!"

Troy and I fist-bumped. He passed me the ball. I took a quick shot and said, "You're back?"

I guess that I could have said something more obvious, but that was what came out of my mouth first.

"You know it."

He slapped me five again.

"What happened?" I asked. "I mean, how—?"

Coach Grady blew the whistle. "Three-man weave," he shouted. "Come on. We have our first scrimmage next Tuesday. Let's get moving."

Troy gave me the full-wattage smile again and said, "Let's talk later. You want a ride home?"

"Sure."

"Okay, man, I'll fill you in then. Let's get to work."

It was a great practice. We had a lot of skilled players, but Troy was the floor leader. He had the experience and the know-how. He was a natural-born leader on the court. No question about it: We were a better team with him back. Practice was more fun. Everything fell into place.

Except for one small thing.

Brandon Foley seemed unusually quiet.

"All okay?" I asked Brandon during a water break.

"Sure."

"Great about Troy."

"Yeah," he said as though spitting out glass. "Great."

I didn't know what to make of him, so I let it go. Troy was

back—and even though I didn't seem to have anything to do with it, my teammates appreciated what I had done. Some even noted that I had been "wronged" in the past and they admired how I "stepped up" in spite of all that.

"Team first," Danny Brown said to me.

"Team first," I agreed.

As practice ended, Coach Grady shouted, "Okay, boys, gather around."

We all took spots on the bleachers. We sucked down water and toweled ourselves off. Troy sat next to me.

"Tomorrow's practice will be at four thirty," Coach Grady said. "We'll be in the other gym for the first half hour, then we move into this one." Coach Grady continued his little spiel, hitting on a few more logistical points. We would be getting our uniforms on Monday, he said. We had the scrimmage in West Orange on Tuesday.

Then he paused and got to the heart of the matter.

"Drug tests for all Kasselton High School winter sports have been declared null and void. It doesn't matter why. All you guys need to know is that we will be running new tests starting in two weeks. Okay, that's it. Young guys, let's get this place straightened up. The rest of you, do your homework and get some sleep."

By "young guys," Coach Grady meant the three juniors and me, the solo sophomore. We were supposed to do the team chores. Some might call it mild hazing, but it wasn't really that. We pulled out the bleachers for the team meetings. We swept the floor at the end of practice. We put the balls back on the rack and locked them up.

Today Brandon helped out. He didn't have to, but as captain, he was that kind of guy. He and I picked up the balls and put them on the rack. Again I couldn't help but notice that he wasn't himself.

"I figured you'd be happy," I said.

"Why's that?"

"You were the one who thought Troy got a raw deal."

He nodded slowly. "I guess I did." Then he looked at me. "Where were you last night?"

"What do you mean?"

"Before you came to my house. Where were you?"

There had been no reason last night to tell him about breaking into the shed. There was even less reason now. "Why?"

"Do you know why they're making us retest?"

I started spinning a ball on my finger. "No."

"Because the old specimens got contaminated."

The ball dropped off my finger. It landed on the floor. The sound echoed in the now-still gym. "How?" I asked.

"Someone broke into the storage center last night."

"What storage center?"

"The town has a storage center where they keep all the drug samples. Last night someone broke into it."

I swallowed. "Where's this storage center?"

"It's in a shed off the circle. Behind town hall."

It was like someone had suddenly encased my arms and legs in cement. "I thought that shed was owned by Buck's father."

"Huh? That's public land. Buck's father has nothing to do with it. It's owned by the town. That's where they keep all the urine specimens—the ones already tested and the backups. But because someone broke in, no one can say if something's been switched or tainted or whatever. That's why they've all been voided."

I staggered back, suddenly dizzy. I could feel the blood rushing to my face. "Do they know who broke in?"

"No," Brandon said. "But the police said it was someone tall."

CHAPTER 44

Troy was waiting for me in the car. He had the same big smile on his face, but now I saw it for what it was. Not friendship. Not sportsmanship or teamwork.

It was the smile of someone mocking me.

I went around to his side of the car. The window was open. I reached in with both hands, grabbed him by the lapels, and pulled him straight out the window.

"What the . . . ?"

"You set me up!" I shouted.

Troy didn't fight back. He just kept smiling at me. "You don't want to make a scene, Mickey."

"You never saw Randy and Buck go into that shed."

"Where's your phone?"

"What?"

"I want to make sure you're not recording this. Get in the car and take your phone out where I can see it."

I wanted to punch him.

Troy pushed me off him, opened his door, and slid back into the car. I was at a loss about what to do.

"You deaf?" Troy asked. "Get in."

I walked back around and got into the front passenger seat of his red sports car.

"Now show me your phone."

I took it out and put it on the console. He checked it to make sure that I wasn't taping the conversation. I wasn't. I should have been, but I wasn't thinking straight. I had let my anger take over. I needed to calm down.

"Is Randy even a drug dealer?" I asked.

"Oh, that part was true," Troy said. "Where do you think I got the steroids?"

So there it was. He'd done them. And I had helped him get away with it—me, the dope who claimed that people could change. Ema had said that they couldn't. Normally I enjoyed irony. Not today.

"I'm going to tell the coaches," I said.

"And what exactly are you going to tell them, Mickey?"

"That we broke into that shed. That I thought . . ."

Troy just kept smiling at me. "Think it through a minute."

I said nothing.

"First off," Troy continued, "you know that the circle has several new security cameras, right?"

"So?"

"So the break-in occurred, according to the police report,

at nine fifteen P.M. When they look through the security footage, are they going to see me leaving the circle heading toward the lab?" He flashed the grin. "Or you—by yourself?"

I remembered now that he had been waiting across the street—on the side of the Y. I had wondered why he had done that, but I never . . .

"Second, if they were to check on my alibi, they'd see that I checked into the YMCA for weightlifting at nine o'clock and checked out again a little after ten. You swipe your card to go in and out. It's all computerized. Oh, they won't know that I turned off the emergency exit alarm, snuck out a side exit, and met you. They'll only be able to confirm that I was at the Y the whole time."

I just looked at him, dumbstruck.

"And, third, there's this cute little video I made with my camera phone. Don't worry. I have copies. If need be, I can send it anonymously to the police or even the media."

It was a short video, just a few seconds—me inside the shed. I remembered now when he came into the room and hit me with the flashlight. I hadn't realized at the time that his video camera was on.

I sat there, feeling numb.

Troy started up the car and pulled out. Danny Brown and a couple of the other guys walked by. Troy waved at them. I didn't.

"It will be your word against mine," Troy said, "and all the physical evidence will back me up. I bet you left fingerprints at the scene, didn't you? I made sure not to touch anything. I stayed hidden when you ran. The police followed you. They know the suspect was tall. I'm not."

I tried to strike back. "But I have no motive."

"Sure you do, Mickey."

"What?"

"You wanted to be the big hero," Troy said. "You wanted to get me back on the team. You're a troubled new kid with no friends and figured this was your way to ingratiate yourself with the popular crowd."

I shook my head. How could I have not seen this coming? But I knew the answer. Troy, in his own horrible way, had nailed it on the head. I had wanted to fit in. Hadn't Ema warned me about that? But I wouldn't listen. I had wanted to be liked. I wanted to be part of the team. I had wanted Troy to be innocent because it would serve my purposes. More than that, I had wanted to be the one to prove him innocent—to be the big hero.

And in the end, Troy was guilty. He had lied and cheated, and now he sat across from me with a big smile on his face.

"So, sure, Mickey, you can tell on me. But think it through. Even if somehow they did believe you—even if they ignored all the physical evidence I have and believed every word you say—well, then what? At best, we both get thrown off the team. You still broke into that storage shed. You can't escape from that fact."

"Wow," I said.

"What?"

"You thought of everything, Troy."

The grin was back. "I don't want to brag but, yeah, I did."

I was trapped. I was searching for an escape route. There was none.

"But it's not all bad," Troy said.

I said nothing. He made a right turn.

"We're teammates now. You saw today how good we can be. We're going to win the states, and now that you have my blessing, the entire team loves you. We are going to win a lot of games together. We are going to celebrate and go far, and then next year, I'll be gone to a top-echelon college and you'll be the new team leader."

Troy stopped the car in front of Uncle Myron's house. He leaned across me and opened the door.

"Cheer up, Mickey. It's all going to be fine. Just be smart about it. See you tomorrow at practice, okay?"

CHAPTER 45

I texted Ema. No reply. I called her. No answer.

I sat at the kitchen table and stewed. Forget her. Hadn't she said that she'd be there when I got hurt from this? She'd known, hadn't she? She tried to make me see what Troy was, but I wouldn't open my eyes. She knew that I'd have to make a big mistake like this and that it would hurt. How had she put it?

I want to protect you from that pain. But I can't. I can only tell you that when it hurts, I'll be there for you.

And then she added, *Always.*

"So where are you now?" I said out loud.

An hour later, Uncle Myron came home. He saw the expression on my face and said, "What happened?"

I wasn't allowed to tell him about Abeona. That was part of the rules. Both Lizzie Sobek and Dylan Shaykes had made that crystal clear to me. But I could tell him about Troy. I could tell him about how my wanting to belong to a team had ruined everything.

Uncle Myron listened with great patience and even understanding. When I finished, he asked one simple question: "Do you know what you're going to do?"

I gave a simple answer: "No."

"Good," he said. "You should sleep on it. Or maybe it's more accurate to say, you should toss and turn on it."

"Yeah," I said. "I don't expect to get much sleep."

"Don't beat yourself up. You messed up. We all do."

"Even you," I said.

It wasn't a question.

"Yeah," Myron said. "I messed up. I thought I was helping your dad all those years ago. It ends up, I made him run away. And, yeah, I know that if I hadn't done that, he'd be alive right now. I live with that ghost every day. And your father isn't my only ghost. There are a lot more who won't let me go."

"Myron?"

"Yeah?"

"How do you live with that?"

"With what, the ghosts?"

"Yeah. How do you live with them?"

"You don't have much choice. What else are you going to do?"

"That's it?" I frowned. "That's your answer."

"Mostly, yeah. And I try to remember that the mistakes I

made were just that. Mistakes. I never meant to hurt anyone. Sometimes you try to do right but wrong still seems to find you. I remind myself of that. And I also remember that it's not the battle, it's the war."

"Meaning?"

"Meaning in the end, I've done more good than evil. I've saved more than I've harmed. You are a sum of your life, not just one part."

I nodded. He started to walk away. "Myron?"

"What?"

"Dad wouldn't want you to blame yourself," I said.

"I know," Myron replied. "And that just makes it harder."

CHAPTER 46

I didn't sleep. But in a little while, none of that would matter.

In fact, what Troy Taylor had done to me wouldn't matter either.

As I grew more tired, delirium started to set in. I saw Troy's mocking grin. Then I saw Luther's mocking grin. Sometimes the smiles were superimposed on top of each other. Sometimes one face slowly transformed into the other.

Luther and Troy. My enemies. My Butchers.

At 6:00 A.M., still lying on my back, I heard the phone ring. Early, I thought.

A few minutes later, I heard the basement door open. Uncle Myron trudged down the stairs slowly. I sat up when I saw his face. It looked like someone had just punched him in the stomach.

"Who was on the phone?" I asked.

"Buck's father."

"What happened?"

Uncle Myron swallowed hard. "Buck."

"What about him?"

"He's dead."

CHAPTER 47

Speed was of the essence, so I asked Myron to drive me to Ema's house.

"Was Ema close to Buck?" Myron asked.

He saw the look on my face, nodded, and grabbed his keys. We sprinted to the car. He gave me details, though it all came to me through a haze. Buck's body was found buried in the woods not far from his father's gym. The news hadn't been released to the media yet. Myron had been called in his "professional capacity."

I wasn't sure what he meant by that.

We reached the front gate. There were two lion heads on either side. Uncle Myron had already called Angelica Wyatt, Ema's mom, so the gate was open. We drove through and up the long hill toward the estate.

"The cause of death is still unknown," Uncle Myron said.

"But he was murdered, right?"

"I don't think so."

In front of us, the huge baronial mansion started to come into view.

"Wait, you said someone buried him in the woods."

"Yes."

"So how could it not be murder?" I asked.

He didn't reply. Or maybe I didn't wait long enough for the answer. We'd arrived. I said, "Stay here," and hopped out of the car. Before I knocked on the door, Angelica Wyatt opened it. I hesitated for a moment. It is odd what star power does to a person. I had only met her in person a couple of times, so seeing her in the flesh, after so many years on the screen, still felt surreal.

Angelica Wyatt crossed her arms and blocked the door. "What's going on?"

"I need to talk to Ema."

"What happened with you two?"

"Nothing. If I could just—"

"She's been crying since she got home."

That slowed me down a second. "She's been crying?"

"All night. She won't say a word to me or Niles. She just"— Angelica Wyatt started welling up too—"cries."

"Does she know . . . ?"

"Know what?"

"Please, I just need to talk to her. Where is she?"

"The basement."

I didn't hesitate now. I knew the way. I ran past her, nearly slipping on the Italian marble floor. I ran toward the kitchen, veered right, found the basement door. I didn't bother knocking. I opened it and started down the stairs.

"Ema?"

The room was dark. There were faint lights above the Angelica Wyatt movie posters. I couldn't see much with it. But I could hear the cries.

Ema was sitting on a beanbag chair. I started toward her, but she put her hand up. "Don't." She looked up and met my eye. The tears were still on her face. She didn't bother to wipe them away. Gone was the heavy makeup, the black lipstick, the temporary tattoos. Ema looked so young right now. She looked young and vulnerable and really, in a way I don't think I ever fully noticed before, pretty.

"I need to tell you something," I said.

"Go ahead. Tell me from there."

I took a deep breath. I had never delivered devastating news like this. I wasn't sure of the protocol, but the fact that she was already sobbing made me rush it. "It's Buck," I said. "He's dead."

I wasn't sure what I expected. I figured that she'd start sobbing again. But that wasn't what happened. Instead she stood and said, "Thanks for letting me know."

I waited.

"That's it?"

She didn't reply.

"You've been crying," I said.

There was something close to anger in her tone. "You're so perceptive, Mickey."

"Why have you been crying?"

Again she didn't reply. She didn't have to. The answer was obvious.

"You knew already," I said. "But how? They just found his body. The media . . ." And then I saw it. "My God. That's what Buck's mother told you, didn't she?"

"She knew who I was," Ema said. "She found Buck's e-mails to me. She knew what I meant to him. And what he meant to me."

"I don't understand."

"She said that she didn't want me to live not knowing the truth. Or thinking Buck had just carelessly broken my heart. But I don't think that was it. I think she needed someone to confide in. So she made me swear never to tell."

"And you agreed?"

Ema nodded. "I agreed."

"And that's why you didn't tell me about it yesterday?"

"No," Ema said. "That had nothing to do with it."

"But you said . . . wait, what did Buck's mother tell you exactly?"

"She talked about how Buck had felt all that pressure. Your buddy Troy added to it. Buck needed to get bigger and stronger. So, yes, he took steroids. A lot of them. And then we met online—and he started to change. But, like Jared said, he was still torn between his two worlds."

I swallowed. "What happened to him, Ema? How did he die?"

"His brother, Randy."

"He killed him?"

"In a sense," Ema said. "Randy thinks he understands how these drugs work. He doesn't. I don't know if Buck had a bad reaction to them. I don't know if he took too many of them accidentally. I don't know if he took too many on purpose."

"He overdosed?"

Her tears came freely now. "Yeah," she said. "He overdosed. He was alone and he shot this stuff into his veins and . . ."

"But his body," I said. "It was buried in the woods. If it was an overdose . . ."

"Think about it, Mickey."

I tried, but it wasn't coming to me.

"The NFL draft was coming up," Ema said. "Randy was already secretly fighting a positive steroid test. If this came out, if they found out Buck had overdosed because of Randy . . ."

I shook my head. My eyes went wide. "Parents would never do that."

"You don't get it."

"What?"

"Of course they would. Buck's mother said it clear as day. Buck was dead. There was nothing they could do for him.

They had another son. He'd lose everything. He'd probably go to jail on drug charges and maybe even for manslaughter. She and I sat at her kitchen table, Mickey. She looked me in the eye and said, 'We lost one son, but we didn't have to lose two. What good would it do to destroy Randy's life too?'"

I couldn't believe it, but it all made a strange, horrible kind of sense. "So they buried Buck's body," I said. "They made up that story about him going to live with his mother. Who'd check a remote island? And even if they did, she could just say, what, Buck was at work or traveling."

Ema nodded. "They hadn't really thought it all out, but eventually she would move overseas. She'd tell people that she and Buck were living in Europe."

"My God. That's awful."

"And yet it would work. Who'd question it? In a horrible way, it's logical and even loving. They couldn't save the one child—"

"So they tried to save the other," I said, finishing the thought.

I thought about what Uncle Myron had said, about the mistakes that cost my father his life, about the ghosts that haunt him even now. "Still," I said. "How do you live with that?"

"I'm not sure that she could."

"So you think, what, you were, like, her confession."

"I think she just needed to confide in someone. She knew I cared about him. She thought that maybe I even loved him. So she told me the truth and swore me to secrecy."

We stood there, feeling the full weight of the moment.

"But now Buck's body has been found," I said.

"Yes."

"Hours after you learned the truth and promised not to tell."

"Yes."

"That's some coincidence," I said.

"No coincidence. You see, that's what Buck's mom didn't count on."

"What?"

"She loved both her sons," Ema said. "But I loved only one." The room grew very still.

"You called the police?" I asked.

"No. I stopped at the library after I left you. I sent an anonymous e-mail to them. I told them where Buck's body was. I told them how he died. I told them the truth. With the clues I gave them, they'll put it all together."

We stood there. Upstairs I heard voices. Myron had come into the house after all. He was talking to Ema's mom. They were right above us. And they were a million miles away. Everyone else was a million miles away. Right now, in this basement, there was only Ema and I and maybe the ghost of a teenage boy who was no longer buried alone in the woods.

CHAPTER 48

By noon, the media was all over the story.

Buck's family was arrested. None were charged with murder. I don't know what the charge is for hiding your own son's body to protect your other son from prosecution. Whatever that was, that's what the parents were both charged with. A search of the house found steroids and other banned substances in Randy's room. I don't know what charges were filed against him, but it sounded like a lot of them.

I only knew that it was over for me. Except, of course, it wasn't.

Not even close.

A week later, Uncle Myron and I went to Buck's funeral.

When we got back to the house, we sat in the kitchen.

We didn't say a word for a very long time. We just sat in

our dark suits and stared into space. Buck was dead. I couldn't believe it. The finality of it was something I still couldn't comprehend.

"So young," Uncle Myron said with a shake of his head. "I know you've heard this before, Mickey, but you always have to be careful. Life can be so fragile."

We sat in silence again. I loosened my tie. Time passed. I can't say how much.

"I know it seems irrelevant now," Myron said. "But do you know what you're going to do about Troy and the basketball team?"

I nodded. "No choice really."

He just waited.

"I'm going to tell Coach Grady the truth."

"The truth will get you thrown off the team," Myron said.

"Too bad," I said.

"It's not the end of the world."

In light of what we had just seen, I knew that was true. But it still hurt.

"There will be next season," Myron said.

I couldn't imagine it right now, but maybe he was right. Or we could move. Mom might be better again. But I couldn't let Troy get away with it. Every basket we'd make would feel tainted. There would be no joy. That was the problem with doing the wrong thing for whatever reasons.

It never feels right.

Uncle Myron opened the fridge and sighed.

"What?"

"We're out of Yoo-hoo."

Myron drank this chocolate soda called Yoo-hoo non-stop. "There's more in the basement," I said. "You want me to get it?"

"No, I'll do it."

He started down the stairs. I was alone. I walked over to the sink. The room was silent. Silent, I thought, as a tomb.

Maybe that was it.

I started thinking now about silence. More specifically, I started to think how silent this kitchen was at this very moment. I looked over at our refrigerator. I started thinking about how Bat Lady's refrigerator was so noisy. I leaned closer toward the sink. Through the pipes, I could hear Myron whistling some old song. So maybe that was it.

Or maybe it was when Myron whistled that song.

Or maybe it was when I realized that I could hear him faintly through the pipes.

Or maybe it was because I realized how quiet our refrigerator was and if it'd been noisy—if it'd been like Bat Lady's—I'd never hear that faint noise.

Especially if I was old. Especially if I played music a lot.

I felt a cold pinprick at the base on my neck.

Bat Lady had turned off the music too. That was what she said. She turned off the music so she could hear the doorbell when the repairman came. Her kitchen had been silent for the first time in years.

Silent. Like this one.

No refrigerator noise. No music.

And that was when she heard the faint sound of my father's voice.

Like I was hearing the faint sound of Myron's.

The cold pinprick grew and spread.

"Oh my God," I said to myself. Then in a panic, I started shouting, "Myron! Myron!"

At the sound of my voice, he ran up the stairs as fast as he could. "What's wrong? Are you okay?"

"Do you have an axe?"

"A what?"

"An axe? An axe!"

"In the garage. Why?"

"Get in the car."

"Where are we going?"

"Just . . . just get in the car."

CHAPTER 49

It was still daylight when we got to Bat Lady's house.

I was out of the car before Myron pulled to a complete stop. I had the axe in my hand. I ran through the crime-scene tape. The tape made sense now. The police hadn't put it up.

Luther had.

He wanted to keep people away.

That was why he set the house on fire too. He wasn't trying to kill Bat Lady or me.

He wanted us gone.

"Mickey? Where are you going?"

Someone had locked the garage door. I took the axe, aimed at the knob, and smashed it open. I found the trapdoor and threw it back.

"Mickey?" Myron said again.

The secret room that had been sealed off all those years—it

was soundproof. That was what Dylan Shaykes had told me. But he also said it had huge food supplies and a shower and a toilet. It had plumbing.

And if you had plumbing, there were pipes.

You couldn't make those soundproof. Sound could always find its way through pipes, no matter how distant and faint.

The dead never speak to me, Bat Lady had said.

Could she be right? Oh please, please, let her be right . . .

I found the hidden door to the sealed secret room. There was no way I was going to bust it open, even with the axe. The door was thick steel. Instead I took the axe and started pounding the dirt just outside the door frame.

I thought about Luther and little Ricky trapped in this room all those years ago.

I thought about him in there watching the only person he ever loved slowly suffer and die.

He blamed my father for that.

What better revenge, I thought, than to lock my father down there alone for the rest of his life?

Uncle Myron was down the ladder now. "What is this place?"

I could hear the awe in his voice. I didn't answer. Seeing what I was doing, Myron ran down the corridor and found a metal bar. He started working on the other side of the frame. I swung the axe until exhaustion. Then I kept going. When I needed one short break, Myron took over.

I pounded on the door. "Hello?"

No reply.

Was I wrong?

I took the axe back. Myron worked with the metal bar.

Finally, after half an hour, I felt the door budge just the slightest bit. That propelled me. Or worse. I may have lost my mind at that stage. I don't know. But I started wielding the axe harder and harder, tears running down my face, my muscles so far beyond exhaustion, I didn't know what would happen next.

"Please," I cried. "Please . . ."

In the corner of my eye I could see Myron watching me, wondering what to do, whether he should grab me and stop my frenzy.

He looked as though he was about to do just that when the heavy door finally gave way.

It fell into the darkened space with a great thud. For a moment, no one moved. Nothing happened. There was no light in the room. I stopped breathing. I dropped my axe, reached into my pocket, and pulled out my phone.

As I switched on the light, I saw a figure rise before me in silhouette.

I lifted the beam toward a familiar face.

My heart stopped.

The face was drawn and bearded, but I recognized it even before I heard Myron gasp out loud.

With my legs shaking, I stepped into the room and managed to say just one word.

"Dad."

EPILOGUE

Ten minutes later, I walked into another dark room.

After I said his name, my father ran to me. I wrapped my arms around him and just collapsed. But my dad held me up. He held me up for a very long time. Pain is a funny thing. It can't endure in the face of hope. Even as my father held me, even as I knew that we weren't out of the woods yet, I could feel so much of my old pain subside. I could feel my wounds closing up as though something divine had touched me.

Maybe it had. What really is more divine than a parent's love?

My father was alive.

For a long time I wouldn't let myself believe it. I held on, afraid to let him go. I just held on tighter and tighter. See, I had been here before, in dreams. I would see my father in my sleep and I would hold him like this, tighter and tighter, and then the dream would start to end and I would shout, "No, please don't go!" but slowly, as I awoke, he would fade.

I'd wake up alone.

Not this time. I held on. And when I finally let go, my father didn't go anywhere.

"Oh my God," Myron shouted, running toward us. The two brothers hugged so hard that they both fell on the floor. Myron cried. We all did. We cried. Then we laughed. Then we cried again. Eventually Myron let my dad go. Then Uncle Myron picked up his cell phone and called my grandparents.

Boy, did that lead to more crying.

My father, Brad Bolitar, had been down in that secret room alone, in the dark, for nearly eight months. But he would be fine. Luther was still out there. But capturing him would wait for another day.

When I met again with Spoon, Ema, and Rachel—when I told them about this amazing discovery—we celebrated. But not for long. Because we also knew the truth.

It wasn't over for the four of us.

We had more questions to answer. We had more children to rescue.

But all of that could wait.

Right now, as my father and I faced each other in that tunnel, there was something that mattered much more to me.

"We have to go," I said to him.

Dad nodded. I think somehow he understood.

• • •

So now we were walking into another dark room. He stayed in the doorway, out of sight. I moved toward her bed.

"Mom?"

My mother looked up and saw the expression on my face. "What is it, sweetheart? What's wrong?"

I choked back the tears. "Remember I said the next time I came back, I was bringing Dad?"

"What? I don't understand . . ."

And then my father stepped away from the doorway and came toward us.

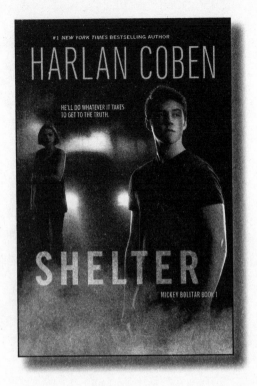

After witnessing his father's death and sending his mom to rehab, Mickey Bolitar has to live with his estranged uncle Myron and switch to a new school. The one saving grace is Ashley, Mickey's new girlfriend. But then Ashley vanishes without a trace. Unwilling to let another person walk out of his life, Mickey follows Ashley's trail to a seedy underworld that reveals that Ashley wasn't really who he thought at all. And neither, it turns out, was Mickey's father. Soon Mickey finds himself caught up in a conspiracy so shocking that it makes everything else in his life look like child's play. . . .

THE EXCITEMENT CONTINUES IN

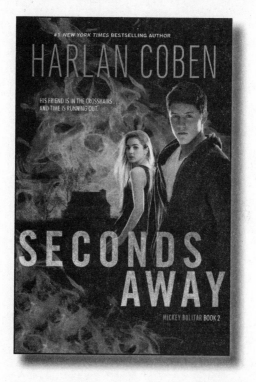

When tragedy strikes close to home, Mickey Bolitar and his loyal new friends—sharp-witted Ema and the adorably charming Spoon—find themselves at the center of a murder mystery involving their friend Rachel. Now, not only does Mickey have to continue his quest to uncover the truth about the Abeona Shelter and the Butcher of Lodz, he needs to figure out what happened to Rachel—no matter what it takes.

Mickey has always been ready to sacrifice everything to help the people he loves. But how can he protect them when he's not even sure who—or what—he's protecting them from?